Eternal guardians ; bk. 8
1001 Dark Nights

Unchained

Also From Elisabeth Naughton

Eternal Guardians
(paranormal romance)
MARKED
ENTWINED
TEMPTED
ENRAPTURED
ENSLAVED
BOUND
TWISTED
RAVAGED
AWAKENED

Firebrand Series
(paranormal romance)
BOUND TO SEDUCTION
SLAVE TO PASSION
POSSESSED BY DESIRE

Against All Odds Series
(romantic suspense)
WAIT FOR ME
HOLD ON TO ME
MELT FOR ME

Aegis Series
(romantic suspense)
FIRST EXPOSURE
SINFUL SURRENDER
EXTREME MEASURES
LETHAL CONSEQUENCES
FATAL PURSUIT

Unchained

An Eternal Guardians Novella

By Elisabeth Naughton

1001 Dark Nights

EVIL EYE
CONCEPTS

Unchained
An Eternal Guardians Novella
By Elisabeth Naughton

1001 Dark Nights
Copyright 2016 Elisabeth Naughton
ISBN: 978-1-942299-55-4

Foreword: Copyright 2014 M. J. Rose
Published by Evil Eye Concepts, Incorporated

Sign up for the 1001 Dark Nights Newsletter
and be entered to win a Tiffany Key necklace.

There's a contest every month!

Go to www.1001DarkNights.com to subscribe.

As a bonus, all subscribers will receive a free
1001 Dark Nights story
The First Night
by Lexi Blake & M.J. Rose

One Thousand and One Dark Nights

Once upon a time, in the future...

*I was a student fascinated with stories and learning.
I studied philosophy, poetry, history, the occult, and
the art and science of love and magic. I had a vast
library at my father's home and collected thousands
of volumes of fantastic tales.*

*I learned all about ancient races and bygone
times. About myths and legends and dreams of all
people through the millennium. And the more I read
the stronger my imagination grew until I discovered
that I was able to travel into the stories... to actually
become part of them.*

*I wish I could say that I listened to my teacher
and respected my gift, as I ought to have. If I had, I
would not be telling you this tale now.
But I was foolhardy and confused, showing off
with bravery.*

*One afternoon, curious about the myth of the
Arabian Nights, I traveled back to ancient Persia to
see for myself if it was true that every day Shahryar
(Persian: شهریار, "king") married a new virgin, and then
sent yesterday's wife to be beheaded. It was written
and I had read, that by the time he met Scheherazade,
the vizier's daughter, he'd killed one thousand
women.*

Something went wrong with my efforts. I arrived in the midst of the story and somehow exchanged places with Scheherazade – a phenomena that had never occurred before and that still to this day, I cannot explain.

Now I am trapped in that ancient past. I have taken on Scheherazade's life and the only way I can protect myself and stay alive is to do what she did to protect herself and stay alive.

Every night the King calls for me and listens as I spin tales. And when the evening ends and dawn breaks, I stop at a point that leaves him breathless and yearning for more. And so the King spares my life for one more day, so that he might hear the rest of my dark tale.

As soon as I finish a story... I begin a new one... like the one that you, dear reader, have before you now.

*"There is the heat of love,
the pulsing rush of longing,
the lover's whisper, irresistible—
magic to make the sanest man go mad."*

—Homer, *The Iliad*

CHAPTER ONE

"Find me. I'm waiting. I'm waiting only for you..."

The words echoed in Prometheus's head as he wandered the empty halls of the ancient castle high in the Aegis Mountains. He heard them in his waking hours now, not just when he was asleep. Heard them tickle the hairs on his nape, heard them whisper like a lover in his ear, heard them call like fire to his blood until he twitched with the need to find her and claim her as his own.

Her. The female with the flame-red hair and eyes like glittering emeralds he'd conjured with his mind. The female who was now more real to him than, well, him.

Damn, but he'd fantasized about her so often over the last few months he wanted her more than he wanted his precious isolation. But the voice wasn't real because *she* wasn't real. Not even a Titan, a god with the power to match that of any ruling Olympian's powers, could make her real. The only person in the cosmos who could summon life was the Creator, and the Creator had screwed Prometheus over so long ago, Prometheus knew there was no chance in this world or the next that he'd ever be blessed with a living version of his endless fantasy.

Life didn't work that way. Correction, *his* life didn't work that way. His life was a series of bad choices and never-ending repercussions. Which was exactly the reason he was determined to stay right here in this dank castle and *not* follow the sultry voice that made him so hard he could barely walk.

He waved a hand, using his telekinetic powers to light a torch along the wall in the cold, dark hallway as he moved. Maybe he was going mad. Maybe all these years of isolation were finally catching up with him. After the Argonauts—warrior descendants of the strongest heroes in all of Ancient Greece—had freed him from Zeus's chains, Prometheus had craved nothing but solitude. To do what he wanted, when he wanted—or to do absolutely nothing at all. But now, more than twenty-five years later, he was starting to wonder if his self-imposed seclusion in this ancient castle was at the root of all his problems. He was hallucinating, for shit's sake. Not just visions, but voices now, too. A sane person didn't do that. A sane person—mortal or immortal—recognized when he was standing on quicksand and got the fuck out.

"Find me. I'm waiting, Titos. I'm waiting for you..."

She always called him Titos in his hallucinations. A nickname that translated to fire. One that now brought him around to stare down the dark and empty hallway even though he knew she wasn't real.

Nothing moved. No sound met his ears. The castle was as silent as it had been since the day he'd arrived. But his spine tingled with apprehension, and his god-sense, something he rarely relied on because no one knew where he was, shot a warning blare straight through his ears.

The witches in the valley at the base of Mt. Parnithia had told him this castle in the Argolean realm had once belonged to an evil sorcerer who'd chosen darkness over light. That sorcerer's quest for power had cost him his life, and he now resided in the lowest levels of Tartarus, tortured endlessly by Hades much as Prometheus had been tortured by

Zeus. His energy still lingered, though. A vile and murky energy Prometheus felt vibrating in his bones. As a divine being, Prometheus wasn't worried that energy would claim him—he was too strong for that—but he couldn't help but wonder if the sorcerer's dark energy was somehow affecting him. Could it be the source of the voice?

"Titos... I'm waiting..."

"Who's there?" he called.

Silence met his ears. His pulse ticked up as he scanned the darkened corridor, the only light coming from the torch behind him. Still nothing moved. Even the wind outside the castle walls had died down as if it too were afraid to utter a sound.

His imagination. It had to be. A hallucination or whatever the fuck he wanted to call it. Frowning, he turned away only to catch a flash of white out of the corner of his eye.

He whipped back. Some kind of gauzy fabric disappeared into the library, followed by the sound of laughter.

Sexy, feminine laughter.

Prometheus's stomach tightened as he rushed to the threshold of the room, grasped the doorframe, and peered inside. Shelves lined with books covered all four walls. A cold, dark fireplace sat across the distance. An empty couch, two side chairs, and a small coffee table lingered in the middle of the library.

Nothing moved inside the room. No fabric rustled. No laughter sounded in the cool air.

His stomach dropped when he realized he was hallucinating again, and he lowered his head into his hand and rubbed his aching temple. What had he said to himself earlier? A sane person recognized when he was standing on quicksand and got the fuck out? Maybe it was time he did that. Maybe it was time he moved on from Argolea and refocused on what he should have been doing these last twenty-five years. Namely, finding a way to screw Zeus over for everything the asshat god had done to him.

"I can help you."

Prometheus's head jerked up at the sound of the sultry feminine voice he'd heard so many times in his dreams. Only this time when he looked the room wasn't empty. This time a gorgeous female with hair as wild as fire and eyes like chipped emeralds peered back at him from the couch.

"I can help you exact revenge on Zeus," she whispered, sitting forward so her breasts heaved in the low-cut white gown. "All you have to do is help me first."

* * * *

"Help you how?" The Titan took one step into the library and stopped. "Who are you? And how did you get here?"

This was where she needed to be careful. Circe slowly pushed to her feet and brushed the thick curls over her shoulder. If he suspected too much, all her efforts would be for naught. She had to play this cool, had to stick to the plan, had to wait for just the right moment to strike.

"My name is Keia." Not entirely a lie, she figured. For thousands of years, humans had called her a goddess pharmakeia, which was just a fancy nickname for witch or sorceress. She was simply borrowing from that label. "But I am not here. I am only an apparition."

"I don't believe you." Prometheus stalked forward. He reached out to grab her but his wide palm and long fingers passed through nothing but air.

His hazel eyes widened as he looked from his hand back to her. "What the hell?"

He was only a few inches taller than her nearly seven feet, but he was bigger everywhere. A wall of solid steel that stood between her and eternity. Power radiated from his broad shoulders and chiseled muscles. A power that made her heart beat faster and her blood warm in a way it hadn't done in ages.

His dark hair was cut short, his jaw strong and square and covered by three days worth of stubble that made him look both dangerous and sexy. He was thousands of years old—like her—but he didn't look a day over thirty. And when his eyes narrowed and his luscious lips thinned, she had an overwhelming urge to dive into his mouth to find out if he tasted as good as he looked.

"How did you find me?" he said. "What do you want with me?"

Circe blinked, his voice pulling her back to the moment. She'd not been sexually attracted to anyone in so long, she'd forgotten what that rush of excitement felt like. Then again, she'd not had the chance to be attracted to anyone. Zeus kept her locked up tight and had for way too long.

Focus. Sexy as hell you can use to your advantage.

She lifted a foot-long length of heavy chain. "Look familiar?"

His face paled as he looked at the chain Zeus had used to bind him to that rock. The rock where he'd been tortured daily by a giant eagle that had torn into his side and consumed his liver day after day. "Where did you get that?"

"Find me and I'll tell you."

His confused gaze lifted to her face. "Find you?"

"You're a Titan. You have powers others don't. Find me and I can help you make Zeus pay for everything he's done."

He glanced over her from head to toe, a careful sweep of his green-brown eyes that was filled with both skepticism and interest. "Who are you?"

She could tell him she was a witch, but instinct made her hold her tongue. Prometheus was wary of all otherworldly beings. Many had known about his torture over the years, but none had dared rescue him from Zeus's clutches. None but the Argonauts.

"I'm no one of importance. Just a maiden who helped another and is now trapped because of it. Much as you were trapped for helping mankind."

Prometheus had given fire to humans. That was the big sin Zeus had punished him for. On a grand scale, she could see how his punishment made sense. Fire had led to the industrialization of man and the advancement of society. Zeus would have preferred man continue to worship and rely on the gods. Circe, on the other hand, had only helped free another of Zeus's prisoners, one who'd already fulfilled his required destiny for the king of the gods. But Zeus was determined to torment her forever for that crime.

She'd learned one very valuable lesson then. If you crossed Zeus you were fucked whether your offense was a major or minor violation.

She had to get out of here. She'd go mad if she had to spend eternity in this prison. Urgency pushed her forward. "Please help me."

"I can't. I don't know how." He looked over her again. "You're nothing but air."

"I—" Footsteps echoed close. Her pulse shot up. Zeus was back. Waving her hand, she broke the feed as she swiveled toward the sound. Prometheus's frantic "Wait," faded in the air as she faced the king of the gods.

Zeus strolled into her cave high on Mount Olympus and stared up the three stone steps where she stood next to the copper cauldron she used to conjure her magic. The flames in the bowl slowly shrank and eventually died out.

His black as night eyes narrowed. He was taller than most gods, over seven feet, and nothing but muscle. And though she supposed some probably found his dark looks attractive, Circe realized he paled in comparison to Prometheus.

"Well?" Zeus asked, hands on his hips and a perturbed expression across his angular face.

"These things take time, my king." She lowered her head in a reverent bow but gritted her teeth because just doing so made her want to scream.

"I grow tired of your lack of progress. I want the water element, and I want it now."

Of course he did. Ever since he'd stolen the Orb of Kronós—the magical disk that housed the four basic elements and had the power to unleash the Titans from Tartarus—from the Argonauts, he'd been pressuring her to figure out where Prometheus had hidden the last element. The god who possessed the Orb with all four elements intact could lord ultimate power over every living being. Forget controlling simply the heavens. With the water element, Zeus would finally control every realm and each being in them.

Circe was determined not to let that happen. Though Zeus was allowing her to contact Prometheus with her powers so she could find the element for him, she was really planning to convince Prometheus to break her free from this hell. Because it was hell. Being trapped in this mountain, even though she was allowed to use her magic, was as much a prison as any other. She was tired of doing what Zeus wanted. Tired of being his yes-witch. Tired of living half a life tucked away from the world.

"My magic cannot be rushed," she said, careful not to give her plans away. "We've discussed this before. You must be patient."

Zeus's jaw clenched down hard. "Do whatever you have to do to get me that element. But you'd better get it quickly because I'm a god of only so much patience. If I don't see results soon, witch, things are going to change."

Circe lifted her chin as he turned to leave. He couldn't threaten her. Because of him, she was the strongest witch who'd ever lived, and he knew that. Oh, she'd get results, but they'd be for her, not him.

When his footsteps faded in the tunnel that led out of her cave, she turned back to her cauldron and bit her lip. She couldn't go on visiting

Prometheus as an apparition. He was already fascinated by her. She needed to step up her game.

A wry smile pulled at her lips as an idea formulated. One that would take him from fascination to obsession and set the wheels of change in full motion.

CHAPTER TWO

Prometheus sat on the top of a knoll in the summer sun, his elbows resting on his updrawn knees, a stalk of wheat between his teeth as he looked across the valley. Sunlight beat down, filtering through the leaves of the oak above. With his enhanced eyesight he could see his daughter Natasa in the field far below, summoning her gift of fire as she entertained the handful of young around her.

Knowing she was healthy and happy warmed a place inside his heart. Because of him she'd endured a very hard life, but the last twenty years had been good to her, and he was thankful for that. She was mated with the Argonaut Titus, and their bond only seemed to be strengthening. They didn't have young of their own yet, but Prometheus knew it was only a matter of time. Natasa loved children, and even though Titus had always been resistant to forging a family, the Argonaut was slowly coming around.

Prometheus watched Natasa form a fireball in the palm of her hand and send it swirling toward the sky. Excitement and glee shown in the eyes of the youthful faces around her. At Natasa's side, Titus smiled and slipped an arm around her shoulder while the young laughed and pointed. No, she might not have young yet, but she would be an incredible mother one day, and Prometheus was bound to be here when that happened.

He sighed as he watched the happy scene. She was the real reason he stayed in this realm. So he could make sure she was safe. So he could watch over her the way he should have watched over her long ago. A paternal urge to join her in that field pulled at him, but he ignored it. His daughter had long ago forgiven him for being the world's shittiest father, but that didn't mean he deserved to be part of her life.

"Find me. I'm waiting. I'm waiting only for you..."

The throaty feminine voice caused Prometheus to turn his head. All other sound drifted to the background as he focused on one thought:

She was back. The mystery apparition from his dreams. The one he'd desperately wanted to touch and taste and devour yesterday in his castle.

"Find me..."

He pulled the stalk of wheat from his mouth, dropped it on the ground, and pushed to his feet. A flitter of white disappeared in the trees.

His heart rate shot up. Like a moth drawn to a flame, he followed, his blood warming with every step. He'd lain awake long into the night rationalizing she was a hallucination. At best, he figured she was a ghost. Either way, he wanted to know why she was haunting him, and there was no better time to find out than right now.

The light faded as he entered the copse of trees. Leaves rustled in the warm breeze. Grass and rocks gave way to a carpet of moss. The rippling edge of white chiffon disappeared behind a tree, the fabric's movement like a lighthouse beacon drawing him home in the dark of night.

He stepped around the trunk of the tree and drew to a stop when he spotted her, standing barefoot in the distance, the straps of the white gown hanging from her delicate shoulders, following the curves at her waist and hips. Ribbons of sunlight filtering through the canopy caught in the fire-red hair spilling down her spine in gentle curls, the color of heat, of flames, of desire and passion.

Slowly, she turned and smiled at him with candy-red lips and eyes that gleamed like emeralds. Her nose was straight with a tiny flare at the tip, her cheekbones high, her skin so pale it looked like newly fallen snow. And even before she spoke he felt himself falling under her wicked spell all over again. The same way he had in his dreams. The same way he did every time he closed his eyes. The exact same way he had yesterday when she'd begged for his help then poofed out of his library with no explanation.

"Who are you?" he whispered, stepping forward.

Her smile faded. "Yours. I'm yours. Find me..."

Her words lingered in the air as she turned and ran.

His adrenaline shot into the stratosphere. "Wait!"

She didn't stop, didn't slow, and without even thinking he pushed his legs forward to follow.

She was fast for a hallucination. His muscles burned as he hustled to keep sight of her through the forest. She weaved her way around brush and trees. A small river rippled somewhere to the right. She darted in that direction, following the meandering water along its bank. He rounded a corner and slowed when he spotted the end of the path. A waterfall loomed ahead, the ground rising on both sides. Past the waterfall, a stone bridge spanned the river, and in the distance, a stately gazebo with marble columns and a domed ceiling overlooked the pristine sight.

Prometheus's breathing slowed as he searched for the female, but he couldn't see her. Long seconds passed with the only sound the water tumbling over rocks. Panic pushed in; panic that he'd lost her, that he'd never see her again, that—

A blur of white rushed across the bridge, moved into the trees, and zigzagged up the hillside toward the gazebo.

His heart kick-started all over again, and he looked toward the cliff ahead. The forest was dark here, but the rocks seemed to form...

Yes, they formed steps leading up the cliff face.

He moved toward the steps, climbing steadily until he reached the top. His legs moved as if they had a will of their own, driving him over the bridge and up the hill until he stood at the base of the gazebo.

It towered above, all ancient stone and marble, with ornate carvings and scrollwork, more temple than garden structure. Energy vibrated from inside, an energy he didn't recognize. Pausing to catch his breath, he stilled and listened to the forest around him, tuning in to his god-sense for any indication of a threat.

"Find me, Titos..."

Her voice slithered over his skin like a sensual caress. Common sense told him to be careful, that he didn't know who or what she really was, but desire pushed his feet up the steps and brought him to a stop at the doorway.

His fantasy stood in the middle of the octagonal room, flame-red hair curling down around her shoulders, gemlike eyes pinned on him, candy apple red lips curved in a wicked, for-his-eyes-only smile.

Forbidden images swept through his mind—the flimsy white gown slipping free of her delectable body, her hands coming up to caress her plump, perfect breasts, a catch of her breath as she slid one hand down her toned belly and into the thatch of red curls at the apex of her thighs.

Blood rushed into his groin, making him instantly hard. A moan echoed in his head...hers, his, he couldn't tell which.

"Come, Titos."

The words were a command he couldn't ignore. He stepped one foot into the gazebo, and another. Her smile grew wider. Heat and the sweet scent of heliotrope surrounded him as he drew close.

"Touch me and make me real."

Yesterday she'd wanted him to find her. Now she was telling him to touch her and make her real. Confusion pulled at his brows. "I don't know how."

She moved closer, until she was mere inches away, and lifted her chest so his attention dropped to her breasts heaving with her breath in the low-cut white dress. "Just touch me. Your Titan powers in this place will do the rest."

His hand lifted as if guided by some unseen force, and as his fingers drew close, he thought he heard her whisper. His gaze darted toward her face, and he watched in a trance as her ruby-red lips moved quickly, the words barely audible.

Ancient Greek. He recognized the tongue, not what she was saying. His hand stilled. Her chanting grew louder. Just as he was about to pull back, she stepped into him, and his fingers passed through what should be her shoulder.

A flash of light illuminated the inside of the gazebo and quickly faded. Prometheus blinked several times and looked down only to realize the warm flesh and solid bones beneath his hand were real.

His gaze darted right back to her face. "Who are you?"

"I told you yesterday. My name is Keia."

She stepped back, away from him, and in a daze he realized the gazebo was no longer dark and empty but illuminated by dozens of candles around the periphery that seemed to have appeared out of nowhere when he touched her. A thick rug made of red and gold swirls lay beneath his feet, a gold chaise with plump red pillows sat ahead. He turned to find two more plush chairs and dozens of soft, luxurious pillows scattered across the floor.

"What just happened?" he asked. "What is this place?"

"You're a Titan." She moved to a small table, uncapped a decanter and poured red liquid into two goblets. Handing him one, she stepped close once more and said, "Don't tell me magic is new to you."

He looked into his goblet as she sipped from her own. Wine, he guessed from the fruity scent, but it might just as well be poison. His gaze narrowed on her flawless features once more. "I'm not in the mood for games."

"Neither am I. You've made me real. In this place, at least. For that I'm thankful." She moved to the chaise and gestured to one of the chairs. "Sit and talk with me for a bit before it's time for me to go. It's been ages since I've had the chance to converse with anyone."

He was having trouble keeping up. And that sweet scent of heliotrope combined with the rich scent of the wine was making him lightheaded. Or maybe *she* was making him lightheaded. He wasn't sure which. "What do you mean before it's time to go? And how are you real here when you weren't at my castle?"

She sighed and lifted her wine to her lips once more. "I suppose an explanation is in order, but there are rules I must abide by. Not all things are allowed to be revealed." She sipped her wine and lowered the goblet to her lap. "I have certain powers."

His eyes narrowed with understanding. "You're a witch."

"Some may call me that. Others call me an enchantress. Regardless of the label, I created this gazebo with my magic. When you touched me within these walls, your Titan powers altered my apparition into flesh. Here I am real."

He wasn't exactly fond of witches. They'd never done anything for him. But magic was a very real thing in their world, and he was in no position to judge. "And when you leave this place?"

"I exist only in this realm in solid form within this gazebo."

He stepped toward her. "I don't understand. You said you were trapped. Who's trapped you? And why—"

"That I cannot tell you, per the rules. What I can tell you is that I've long been fascinated by you, Prometheus. You were watching the Argoleans in the field earlier. Do you have the same affection for them as you do humans?"

She was switching topics way too fast. "Watching me, how?"

"With my magic, of course. It gives me the ability to look through windows. I do a lot of looking because of my confinement. What do they call it in the human realm? Oh yes. People watching." A faraway, almost sad look filled her eyes. She shook her head and blinked several times, a weak smile curling the edges of her plump lips. "I much prefer being real with you here than watching you through that window."

He sat beside her on the chaise, close enough to feel her heat surround him, but not quite close enough to touch. Though he wanted to touch her. He was itching to run his hand over her bare shoulder again. To slide his fingers through her luxurious hair. To pull her in and find out for himself if her lips were as soft and tempting as they looked. "Why me?"

Her smile widened as she turned to face him, and this close...gods, she was more beautiful than he'd expected. Her flawless features took his breath away.

"My, but you are full of questions," she said.

Realizing he probably sounded like a ten-year old, he frowned. "I guess you could say it's been a while since I've had anyone to talk to as well."

"That's why I've been watching you. Because we are so similar." She sipped her wine again. "You didn't answer my question about the Argoleans. In the field."

All he wanted to do was go on peppering her with questions about why she was here, why she'd come to him, and how he could make her stay. But there was something about her... Something that made his pulse tick up and his body feel alive in a way it hadn't in thousands of years. And if she had to leave soon—for whatever reason, he didn't want to waste what little time they had left frustrating her, or him.

"The male in the field was an Argonaut. The female with him was my daughter."

Keia's eyes narrowed in question, then slowly relaxed as if she'd suddenly made connections in her mind. "Ah yes, your daughter. I almost forgot you had a daughter. And her mother? Are you—"

He shook his head. "A one time thing. She died thousands of years ago. She was a nymph who came across me during my imprisonment and eventually went on to marry an Egyptian prince."

"Io?" A knowing light filled Keia's eyes. "Your daughter's mother was Io? I didn't realize that."

He nodded. This witch knew more about him than he'd thought. A voice in the back of his head warned him to be wary but he ignored it. "I didn't even know Natasa existed until several years ago. Because of me, she suffered greatly. I'm in this realm because she's here. Watching out for her is my way of...I don't know, making up for a little of the pain I caused her."

"That's a very fatherly thing to do."

He frowned. "Don't get any ideas. I'm not a good father. Not even close."

"I'm sure you're a better father than you think."

He huffed, lifted his wine. Paused when it was an inch from his lips and stared down into the goblet.

The sweet sound of feminine laughter floated around him. "Worried that cup is poisoned?"

His gaze slid her direction, and he caught the playful gleam in her eyes and the soft spray of freckles across the bridge of her nose he hadn't noticed earlier. "I'd be lying if I said the thought hadn't cross my mind."

Smiling, she leaned forward and took the goblet from his hand, her slim fingers grazing his in the process to send sparks of electricity all through his arm. "Watch, Titos."

She brought his cup to her mouth and sipped, her eyes locked on his the entire time. Lowering the goblet, she licked the droplet of wine from her bottom lip, then bit down gently with her top teeth until the succulent flesh darkened.

Heat spread through his whole body and shot into his groin, bringing his cock to life in a way it hadn't been alive in thousands of years.

"See?" She handed the wine back to him. "No poison. Just decadent pleasure."

He grew hard at the sexual innuendo, but there was still just enough common sense left in his head to make his eyes narrow. "Maybe it doesn't affect you. You did say you were created from magic."

"No, I said magic made me flesh and blood in this place so we could be together." She leaned forward again, drawing his attention right to her delectable cleavage. "I assure you I am a living, breathing female in another realm, not just a figment of your imagination."

Her eyes were hypnotic, her voice sultry and so damn erotic he could go on listening to her talk about anything. Somehow he pulled his attention away from her perfect breasts and looked deep into her emerald eyes. "What realm? Tell me where you are flesh and blood at all times so I can find you."

"That would break the rules. And if we are to see each other again, I can't break them. As for what I want, though..." Her breaths grew shallow as she drew even closer and her gaze dropped to his lips. "I think this want burning inside me is the same one that brought you to this place."

Her hand landed against the back of the chaise, and she angled her face up toward his. The heat of her body surrounded him, consumed him, infused him with need. He lifted his hand to her neck, felt the soft, silken flesh beneath his fingers, and was powerless to hold back.

His mouth lowered to hers as if they were magnets, drawn together by a force neither could resist. Her supple lips brushed his...warm, sweet, tender yet intoxicating at the same time. He had an overwhelming urge to take her, to claim her, to make her his own, but he didn't want to do anything to spook her, and he was still so confused about what and who she was. So he kissed her slowly. Slid his fingers into her sleek hair. Held back from the passion he wanted to release.

She sighed against him. Brought one hand up to rest against his chest. Warmth circled the spot, shot sparks of electricity straight into his groin. Sliding his tongue along the seam of her lips, he coaxed her to open, to let him in, to give him a taste of what he'd been dreaming about for far too long.

She drew back quickly, breaking their kiss before he was ready. His hand dropped to her thigh as she looked to her right.

He didn't care about whatever animal outside the gazebo had distracted her. He only wanted more. He reached for her. "Keia."

"He's back." She pushed to her feet before he could kiss her again. Her gaze stayed locked on something to her right. "What is he doing back so soon?"

"He who?" A little of Prometheus's lust faded when he saw the worry rushing over her features. He stood and reached for her. "Keia?"

She glanced his way. But this time he didn't see heat in her gemlike eyes. He saw fear. True fear. "He's not alone. I have to go."

"Wait." He stepped toward her. "Tell me where you—"

His fingertips grazed her sleeve, but she vanished before he could grasp her.

* * * *

Circe extinguished the flames in her cauldron just as three of Zeus's Sirens—his Barbie-doll like warriors, dressed in skintight black tops, fitted black pants, and knee-high kickass boots—moved into her cave and spread out around her.

"What is the meaning of this?" Circe straightened her back and looked past the Sirens toward the tunnel. "Where is Zeus?"

"Zeus is busy," the one in the middle with blonde hair falling in waves to her shoulder blades said. "He sent us to inspire you."

The brunette to Circe's right chuckled and ascended the steps toward her.

"Stay back." Circe lifted a hand, a chant growing in her mind, but the Sirens moved with stealth speed and were on top of her before she could summon a spell.

They jerked her arms behind her back. "No chants for you," the redhead said, clamping metal cuffs around her wrists. "Not right now anyway."

Circe grunted as the weight of the cuffs pulled on her wrists. But more than that, she felt the power in the metal. Adamant, she realized. The strongest metal in all the realms. A groan echoed from her chest.

"That's right," the Siren to her right said, pushing her forward so she stumbled down the steps. "These cuffs were forged by Hephaestus himself. Your spells won't work so long as they bind you."

They led her out the tunnel from which they'd come. The adamant cuffs didn't just block her magic, they made it impossible for her to fight back. Sunlight spilled into the cave as they grew close to the opening, and Circe tensed. Zeus had trapped her in this cave with his powers. She couldn't leave. If she tried to cross into the light, an invisible force field would jolt her back with an electrical current. The Sirens didn't lead her into the light, though. They turned just when she was sure she was going to be zapped and drew her into a tunnel she'd never noticed before.

Darkness surrounded them. The tunnel circled down into the depths of the mountain. Unable to struggle, Circe followed, unsure where they were leading her. The air grew cold. Ahead, a flickering orange light beckoned.

Unease rolled through her. She'd never been in this part of the mountain, but the hairs on her nape standing straight told her whatever was down here could not be good. The ground finally leveled out as they entered a large room. The Sirens at her back drew her to a stop. The one at her front crossed toward a lone torch lit on the far wall, removed it from the holder, and walked back toward Circe.

The Siren tipped her head. "Zeus has decided you need a little something to inspire you to work harder." Her gaze skipped past Circe. "Ladies?"

The Siren on Circe's right let go of her and stepped away, into the darkness. Metal groaned, and in a heartbeat of understanding, Circe realized the sound was a door opening. A rusted, metal door. And this wasn't just a cave. It was a dungeon.

The Siren at her left maneuvered her into the darkness.

"Wait." Circe tried to push back with her weight, but the adamant cuffs stopped her momentum.

They shoved her into the cell. One uncuffed the manacles from her wrists. The other lifted her boot to the small of Circe's back and thrust her forward.

Circe lifted her hands just before she hit the hard rock wall of the cell. Metal groaned and clanked. Whipping around, Circe spotted the three Sirens standing outside her cell, the one in the middle holding the torch to shine light all around them.

"Don't waste time trying to conjure a spell to free yourself," the brunette said. "These walls are infused with adamant as well. Your powers won't work here." She looked to the redhead, and then the blonde. "We should go before he wakes."

"Wait." A bolt of fear shot down Circe's spine, and she rushed to grasp the bars. "He who?"

The brunette smiled. "You'll find out. Come on, girls."

The light faded along with their footsteps. Darkness pressed in, stealing the air from Circe's lungs. Shivering, she stepped back, holding out her hands until she felt the cold stone wall at her back.

"Don't freak out," she said aloud to keep the fear at bay. "Zeus is just trying to scare you. He'll let you go in a few hours."

A roar sounded outside her cell. Circe's gaze jerked in that direction, and her pulse shot into the stratosphere.

That didn't sound like a Siren. Or a god. It sounded like a monster.

She swallowed hard and told herself the adamant in the bars of the cell door would protect her from whatever was out there. But a clicking sound echoed close. Like nails clawing at the ground. Growing faster. Louder. Coming closer...

She held her breath and went completely still.

The heavy steel door of her cell crashed open. Circe swallowed her scream and slid down the wall, arms and legs shaking, hoping she blended into the darkness

Something drew in a long sniff and growled. "I smell you, witch."

All she saw was the whites of its eyes before it lunged.

CHAPTER THREE

Circe's cell door clanged open hours later. Footsteps sounded across the stone floor. Too weak to lift her head, she groaned and pried her eyelids open only to wish she hadn't.

Torchlight filled the room. A Siren scrunched her nose in distaste as she held the torch and waited in the doorway while the king of the gods crouched in front of Circe and brushed the blood-matted hair away from her face.

"Gesenius was extra rough with you." Zeus clucked his tongue. "Looks like you fought back. Bad idea, witch. A shade is nothing to mess with."

A shade. A death shadow. That's what had attacked her. She would have realized that sooner but the pain had been too great to think through.

"He liked you," Zeus said. "Then again, your blood turned him back into a human for a day. Who wouldn't like you?"

Sickness rolled through Circe's stomach. She closed her eyes again, not the least bit interested in his gloating. Her body was too busy trying to repair itself from the shade's damage.

"Oh now, don't be like that," Zeus said. "You brought this on yourself, Circe. We had a good thing going until you decided to take your own sweet time. Lucky for you I'm a forgiving god."

He wasn't forgiving. He had no intention of living up to his "deal," and she knew that now. He was never going to release her from his service because she was now the most powerful witch in all the cosmos. And to him, she was nothing more than a prize, just as Prometheus had been his prize so long ago.

Prometheus...

He was her only chance now. She had to find a way to convince him to free her completely. And the only way to do that was to make him so obsessed with her, he had no other thought but to come after her.

She needed to move up her timeline. Needed to work faster. Needed to seduce Prometheus now rather than later.

But first she had to get out of this cell so she could get back to her magic.

Groaning, she pushed up on her hands, cringed at the pain in her neck and down her side, but somehow found the strength to shift so she leaned back against the wall. Her dress, damp with blood, fell open across her breasts but she didn't bother to fix it. "What do you want?" she asked, her voice raspy and weak.

"I want that element, witch."

Lead him on. Tell him what he wants to hear.

"I could have gotten it...for you. But your Sirens...interrupted me."

"No, my Sirens clearly inspired you." Zeus's dark eyes narrowed. "You need to work smarter." He brushed another lock of bloody hair back from her cheek, almost tenderly. "I told you I was a patient god, but I have limits." His licentious gaze drifted over her ripped gown and exposed flesh. "Either get me the results I want, or the hell you just lived through will be your new normal." His gaze lifted back to her face. "The clock is ticking, witch."

He rose and looked toward the Siren. "Move her into a cell where she can work. Bring her food and new supplies. Then send someone to clean up this mess. It stinks like death in here."

He stalked out of the room, followed by a smug-looking Siren. Closing her eyes once more in the dark as the metal door clanged shut, Circe shuddered against the cold stone floor.

Your new normal...

Understanding sent bile sliding up her throat. He was going to torture her the same way he'd tortured Prometheus. Painfully. Horrifically. Daily until she gave him what he wanted. And when she did, he might free her from the shade, but he'd never free her from her imprisonment.

Breathing in and out slowly, she fought to regain her strength for one blinding purpose.

To find Prometheus. Because he truly was her last hope.

* * * *

A thick fog covered the forest floor in the dead of night, illuminated only by a sliver of moonlight filtering through the thick foliage above. A shiver raced down Prometheus's spine as he scanned the dark trees that looked almost ghost-like in the dim light.

She was out here. Somewhere. He'd heard her voice in his head. Always calling him. *"Find me, Titos..."*

His heart raced as he stepped forward, his boots disappearing in the fog, his god-sense on high alert. An owl cried above. The high-pitched chirp of bats flying in the distance echoed to his ears. He knew she was out here. Had felt her. The shiver told him something else was out here too. A faceless danger he couldn't see but which hunted her.

A flutter of white darted through the trees. He whipped in that direction, his pulse going stratospheric.

He pushed his legs into a run, darting around eerie gray tree trunks in the forest, jumping over logs and boulders his god-sense picked up beneath the fog. The ground rose steadily upward. His muscles burned as he ascended the hillside. The trees slowly dissipated the higher he ran, finally opening up until he stood on a long flat plateau of rock high above a valley.

Keia stood at the edge of the cliff, overlooking the valley and its meandering river, her thin white gown blowing in the gentle breeze, her fire-red hair fanning out behind her. His breaths came fast and shallow as he slowed his steps, as he tried to figure out why she'd lured him here.

"Keia?"

She turned and faced him, her eyes as green as he'd ever seen them, her face as pale as the moon. "Find me, Titos."

His pulse beat strong and fast, and he stepped toward her. She wasn't real. He knew she wasn't real. She was only real in the gazebo. But he reached for her hand regardless. Then sucked in a breath when his fingers curled around solid flesh and bone.

His gaze dropped to her hand then up to her face. "What's going on? Why did you bring me here?"

She closed both of her hands around his and squeezed so tight pain shot up his arms. "Because you are mine."

Her eyes shifted. They were no longer the color of shimmering emeralds but morphed to hard black cinders. And her voice...it was different. Deeper. Masculine. A voice he'd heard long ago.

She stepped back to the edge of the cliff and pulled him with her. "And you will always be mine, Titan."

The ground fell away. Prometheus's body sailed over the edge. Before he could release her, the ground rushed up at what felt like a million miles per hour.

Prometheus sat upright in a puddle of sweat, the sheet tangled around his legs, his heart racing as his gaze darted around his dark bedroom suite.

No sound met his ears. No voices. His gaze angled down, to the mattress beneath him, to the floor, and finally the window that looked out into the darkness.

Not a cliff. He was in bed, not falling to his death. Not that a Titan could be killed by conventional means, but it *was* possible. Especially where magic was involved.

Magic...

Keia...

That voice...

He knew that voice. It was Zeus's voice. The god who'd imprisoned him and left him to a daily torture that still haunted his restless hours. Throwing his legs over the side of the bed, he drew in deep breaths that did little to settle his racing pulse, let them out slowly, tried to make sense of the dream.

No, not a dream. A warning. His god-sense was picking up something...something he needed to key into before it was too late.

Urgency pushed him across the floor. He pulled on jeans and a T-shirt, shoved his feet into boots, and moved for the dark corridor that led to the stairs. He didn't care that it was the dead of night. Didn't care that common sense was telling him it had just been a dream. He knew what he'd felt, and his senses were going apeshit over the threat he knew lurked somewhere out there in the dark.

He made his way into the trees. A low fog hovered over the ground as he headed toward the gazebo Keia had lured him to only yesterday. Moonlight slanted through the canopy to illuminate the woods in an eerie white glow. Déjà vu trickled through him, but he fought it back and pushed onward. He could flash to the gazebo—he had the power to flash in any realm—but didn't because if danger really did lurk in that magical place, he wanted to surprise it. Minutes later he crossed the bridge and moved silently through the trees toward the dark structure.

Nothing moved inside. No light, no sound came from within its walls. The gazebo was as eerily quiet as the air. He listened, didn't pick up anything out of the ordinary with his heightened senses, but knew not to drop his guard. Magic could cloak danger just as magic could create an alternate reality. Moving silently up the gazebo's steps, he stood at the threshold and peered into the dark room.

The chaise, the pillows, the dozens of candles—now dark—were just as he'd left them yesterday after Keia had disappeared. He stepped into the gazebo and looked over each item, searching for something—anything to explain the warning echoing in his head. Still, nothing stood out.

His heart rate slowed. And little by little the tingles across his spine lessened. It had just been a dream. Brought on by hallucinations, not enough sleep, and impending madness. His years of isolation were taking a toll on him. He turned to leave, was at the point of believing he'd made the whole thing up—even Keia—when he spotted a pool of blood on the floor to his right.

He kicked a pillow away, crouched near the puddle, and slowly touched the edge of the blood.

Electricity shot into his arm, across his chest, and up his neck. Blinding pain radiated outward from the left side of his throat, knocking him off his feet to slam against the ground.

He gasped and quickly swiped his bloody fingers against his pant leg. The pain slowly lessened until it was nothing but a twinge in his flesh.

Reality and fantasy intermingled in his mind until he didn't know which was which. And in the distance he heard Keia's voice calling to him.

"Find me, Titos. Find me before it's too late..."

* * * *

By daybreak, Circe's strength had returned enough so she could conjure her magic. She wasn't a hundred percent yet, but she couldn't wait until her body completely healed. Zeus had made it clear the shade could return at any moment. She needed to step up her plan with Prometheus if she had any hope of breaking free from this prison.

She placed the length of chain Zeus had given her in the cauldron, held her hands over the bowl, and summoned her spell. The chain was her link to Prometheus. It had been a part of him so long it still possessed part of his lifeblood. With it, she could find him wherever he was in the cosmos. And with it she could make herself ethereal and lure him to her.

The rock walls around her faded, revealing stone columns and the sound of leaves rustling in the early morning breeze, birds chirping in the forest, and water rushing over the falls. The scents of moss and wood filled her senses as she turned, confused why the spell had brought her to the gazebo already. She wasn't supposed to start out here. She was supposed to start with Prometheus and tempt him to follow her to th—

The thought halted when she caught sight of him, lying on his side on the chaise, his hands tucked up near his face, his eyes closed, and his chest rising and falling with his deep breaths. Something beneath her ribs tightened at the sight of him. Something other than lust. Fast asleep, his long dark lashes feathering the skin beneath his eyes, he looked more innocent than godly, more angelic than dangerous. And for a fleeting moment she pictured him chained to that rock in the blistering sun, unable to move, unable to do anything but wait for the giant eagle to swoop down and rip out his liver only to come back and do it all again the next day.

He'd only escaped that living hell because of the Argonauts. Because his daughter's mate had rescued him so Prometheus could save her life. Zeus had been pissed when Prometheus was freed. Circe remembered all too well how he'd marched into her cave and ordered her to bring Prometheus back. It had taken her several hours to convince the king of the gods that her witchcraft didn't work that way.

Luckily—for her—Zeus had finally abandoned that order, but she knew he was waiting for the moment when he could make Prometheus suffer. Zeus's memory was long. When someone bested him, he never forgot. And Prometheus had bested him more than any other.

Was Zeus planning something she didn't know? Was he using her as bait? Circe was well aware that the king of the gods wanted the water element more than anything else, but he also always had an agenda. Was Prometheus at risk because of her?

His eyes fluttered open and held on hers. And that tightness beneath her ribs rolled and swirled as he stared at her as if seeing her for the very first time.

He pushed up on his hand, dropped his legs over the edge of the chaise, and blinked several times. Sunlight slanted through the arches to highlight his hair and the dark scruff across his jaw, making him even more handsome than yesterday. He was dressed in jeans and a black T-shirt that pulled across his chest, and when he moved she caught the flex of muscle in his arms. Suddenly, she couldn't help but wonder what his carved shoulders and toned body looked like under all that fabric.

"Keia," he said in a voice still thick with sleep. "You're here."

"I'm here," she repeated, growing hotter with every passing second. She moved toward him. Pain echoed across her neck and shoulder, but she bit back the wince so he wouldn't see. Lowering herself to the chaise, she sat beside him, close, but not too close. Not yet anyway.

He turned to face her, confusion darkening his eyes. "I was looking for you."

Her plan was working. A coy smile twisted her lips as she brushed a hand down the bodice of her green dress, the one she'd conjured to match her eyes and make them appear even darker. "I like that you were looking for me. I came here to find you as well."

"I saw it in the night. Blood. And pain."

Circe's smile faded, and a tingle of apprehension shot down her spine.

"You were scared," he went on. "I tried to help you. But when I reached you, you grasped my wrists like chains, and a voice that was not yours fell from your lips as you pulled me over a great cliff."

Circe's heart beat hard and fast, killing whatever arousal she'd felt earlier. "Who's voice did you hear?"

"Zeus's."

Circe's fingers shook as she pushed to her feet, crossed to the edge of the room and stared out at the water rushing toward the falls. Zeus's voice. How could he have heard Zeus's voice?

Fabric rustled at her back. "What's going on? You said you were trapped. Who has trapped you and why?"

Her mind spun. She couldn't come right out and tell him. Not yet, anyway. He was on the verge of becoming obsessed with her, but he wasn't there yet, and if she revealed too much too soon, she risked losing him altogether.

She had to play this strategically. Had to be smart. Fixing an amused smile on her face, she turned his way. "It sounds like a dream."

"It was a dream. But it was also real. The blood was real, right here on the floor of this gazebo."

He held out his arm, and Circe's gaze followed until she spotted the dark stain on the wood floor. Her breath caught.

"I touched it," he said in a low voice. "I felt it."

Her gaze darted to his features, and in his eyes she saw truth. Through her blood he'd felt her pain and suffering.

He stepped toward her, eyes dark and very focused. "Tell me what's going on here."

"I..." Words faltered on her tongue. She didn't know what to say. Didn't know how any of this was possible. Her two worlds were not supposed to converge. Magic kept them apart. "It wasn't my blood," she lied. "Some kind of animal must have wandered in and—"

His big hands closed around her biceps. "Zeus is involved with whatever's going on with you, isn't he?"

"I don't... I can't... There are rules."

"Fuck his rules. What does he want from you?"

"He wants..." *Don't tell him the truth.* "He wants to punish me."

"Why?"

"Because..." *Think, dammit!* "Because I helped someone."

That wasn't a lie. She had helped someone. When the princess of Argolea had snuck into Olympus and come to Circe in her cave a few months ago, Circe had helped the female find an Argonaut Zeus had imprisoned. Zeus had been pissed when he'd discovered how Circe had betrayed him. Was still pissed. And Circe knew that was part of the reason Zeus was stepping up his pressure on her now to find the water element. But she couldn't tell Prometheus that because his daughter was mated to an Argonaut. If Prometheus was at all privy to what the Argonauts were up to, telling him that would give away who she was, and he might turn away from her for good.

"Someone Zeus was using so he could gain more power," she went on, figuring that was a safe explanation. "I didn't want to help Zeus but I had no choice. He's the king of the gods. When one is in his service, one cannot just say no. I might not age because of my powers, but I'm not immortal like the gods. If Zeus wanted to kill me, he could."

Prometheus's shoulders relaxed, but he didn't let go of her arms, and she liked his hands on her. Liked the warmth of his skin against hers and the way he made her feel small. "The gods can't take life. That goes against the natural order."

She frowned. "They can dictate it though. He keeps me isolated from others. I'm allowed to use my magic—which is how I found you—but that is the extent of my freedom."

She wanted to add that her freedom was limited by what Zeus allowed her to do. She could watch anyone through her mirrors, but she couldn't contact friends or family—not that she had any anymore—without an object linked to their lifeblood. But, of course, she couldn't tell Prometheus that either because then he would know Zeus was aware she was contacting him now, and he'd grow suspicious.

Gods, her life was one major lie after another. Frustration bubbled through her. Frustration and anger and...helplessness.

"Why did you find me?"

Warmth crept up her neck and into her cheeks, distracting her from thoughts of Zeus, from frustration over her imprisonment. Part of what she was about to say was a lie, but truth also lingered in her words. A truth she wanted him to hear. "Because you captivated me. You survived thousands of years of torture at the hands of your enemy, and you didn't just survive it, you came out whole and sane on the other side. I needed to see for myself that was possible."

Unease passed over his features as he let go of her arms, and she tried to fight the disappointment the loss of his touch caused but couldn't mask it completely. "I'm not whole. And I'm not anywhere close to sane."

Panic pinched something in her chest. A panic that came from the reality that he honestly believed what he was saying. She moved closer. "Yes, you are. And you're a hero. As much a hero as any of those Argonauts in the capital city far below us."

He scoffed.

"It's true." And this time there was no lie in her words. "I watched, from my mirror, when you helped the Argonauts twenty-some years ago. I saw how you risked yourself to save your daughter. You were willing to face Zeus, to do anything to save her, even knowing you might be chained again, all because you believed what you were doing was right. I want to be like that." She shrugged, thinking back over the hundreds—no, thousands—of things she'd done in her lifetime for no one's gain but her own. "I wanted to know what that felt like. For once."

His gaze narrowed and held on hers, and as he studied her, she felt as if he were looking all the way inside her, right to the edge of her soul. "How did you end up with Zeus?"

Truth was a bitter pill to swallow, but she didn't want to lie anymore. This, at least, she needed to be honest about. "A long time ago, Zeus made me an offer I couldn't refuse. To amplify my abilities so I would become the strongest witch in all the realms. I took it, thinking my powers would grow. But what I didn't know then was that the king of the gods was playing me. The offer came with a catch. My powers did grow, but only in the cave where I'm confined. By the time I realized what he'd done, it was too late. I was trapped."

"So you exist in that cave—"

"No longer doing what I want, only what he commands. And over the last thousand years I've come to realize that what he wants is ultimate power. Much as I did, only the difference is he has no conscience about the things he orders me to do, and I've developed one. Power means nothing if it's used for evil instead of good."

He stared at her a long beat before saying, "I've often felt the same, which is why I rarely use my powers unless a situation is dire."

"I know." That too was true. She'd learned a lot from watching him. Learned what she should be. She moved closer still, until his heat and heady scent of pine and something citrusy surrounded her. "I was not always a good witch, Titos. But I want to be one. I hope you believe that."

His gaze skipped over her features. "I'm not sure what to believe when it comes to you. You're doing something to me. Something I don't understand."

Her heart beat faster. It was exactly what she needed to hear to put her plan in motion, but that wasn't why her stomach was tingling and heat was suddenly rushing low in her belly. No, this excitement came from knowing he felt the same things she did. "You're doing something to me, too. Something I like far too much."

Her fingers drifted to his forearm, barely grazing the dark hairs and the strong muscles beneath his skin. And when she saw the way his eyes darkened and his breaths picked up speed, that warmth slid down between her legs to send tingles all across her sex.

"You're the only thing I have to look forward to, Titos," she whispered, running her fingertips up his arm to his thick, muscular biceps. "I know it's not fair to you, but I think about you all the time. Even when I shouldn't."

"You do?"

She nodded. "Do you think about me?"

"Far too much."

Her lips curled. And her fingers continued to trace a lazy pattern against his scintillating flesh. She moved closer, until only a whisper of breath separated their bodies and heat was all she felt. "Do you think...? I mean, I know it's probably bold of me, but would you mind if I kissed you again? It's been ages since I felt—"

He moved so fast she barely saw him. One minute he was staring at her with lust-filled eyes that she knew had to mirror her own, and the next his mouth was on hers, making her breath catch, making her body tremble, and her heart race like the wind.

His hands captured her face, slid into her hair, and when he groaned against her, she opened to him, drawing his tongue into her mouth and his heat and life deep into her soul.

He tasted like mint. Like heaven. Like sin and paradise all rolled into one. And she was desperate for more. Desperate to touch and taste and know him as no one ever had. Desperate to lose herself in him for as long as she could before reality dragged her back to the abyss.

His tongue stroked against hers, inundating her with long, wet, deep kisses she felt everywhere. Her breasts grew heavy, her nipples tight, and an ache built between her legs, one she knew only he could assuage.

Groaning into his mouth, she moved closer, until their bodies were plastered together from chest to knee, and his growing erection pressed hard against her belly.

Gods, she wanted him. More than she could ever remember wanting anyone in her 2200-year life. She hadn't lied. She'd been a conniving witch before Zeus had trapped her on Olympus. She hadn't cared who she'd hurt in her quest for power. She'd seduced immortals who could grant her extra powers, then tossed them aside when their usefulness to her was spent. And she would have done the same to Zeus if he hadn't double-crossed her. But imprisonment had taught her a very valuable lesson. That all life had value. And when she'd stopped scheming, she hadn't even missed sex or companionship. Until now.

"Keia..." He whispered her name as he changed the angle of their kiss, as his hands slid down her hair, over her shoulders, and along the length of her spine.

Keia. His whispered word penetrated her hazy mind as his hands reached her waist and he pulled her tighter to him. Not Circe. Not her name. He didn't even know who she was. He was falling under her spell, and she was letting him. A spell she'd cast for her own gain, just like all the other spells she'd cast before her imprisonment.

Her hands drifted up to his shoulders and over to his pecs, and she groaned at how hard and carved he was beneath her palms, but she told herself not to be distracted. Somehow she found the power to push against him and step back, breaking the kiss she only wanted to get lost in.

His face was flushed as he looked down at her, his lips swollen from her mouth, his eyes glazed and so close to gone. "What's wrong?"

"I..." Her heart cinched down tight, sending pain rippling along her ribcage. A pain she'd never felt before, not even when that shade had attacked her.

She had to tell him the truth. She couldn't go through with this lie.

If she did, she was no better than Zeus. If she did...it meant she'd not learned a single thing in the thousand years she'd been trapped on Olympus.

"I can't—"

The unmistakable sound of claws scratching against stone sounded somewhere close, shooting Circe's pulse into overdrive. She darted a look to her left, not seeing the gazebo or forest but seeing the bars of her cell in the bowels of Olympus.

"Keia?"

"I have to go," she said quickly, stepping further away from him. "I can't stay any longer."

She broke the feed and swiveled toward the sound. Prometheus's frantic "Wait," faded in the air. The gazebo dissipated. Dank rock walls appeared around her. She jerked back, knocking the bowl she'd been using to conjure her magic from the pedestal in the middle of the room. It clattered against the hard stones. The flames snuffed out. Hot, red cinders scattered across the floor and paled until they were nothing but cold black coals.

Her heart raced as she flattened her body against the rocks and prayed he moved past, that today she'd be spared.

Her cell door clanged open. She closed her eyes and held absolutely still, knowing there was no use in fighting. Remembering when she'd struggled yesterday and the blinding pain that had followed.

Before she had time to conjure a protection spell, he snarled and lunged. His big body slammed into hers, knocking her head against the hard stones. Pain ricocheted across the back of her skull. Even though she told herself not to, she tensed and cried out. His fangs sank deep into her throat, ripping through her flesh.

She somehow forced herself to relax so he wouldn't tear her to pieces. As the shade feasted on her blood, tears streamed down her cheeks. Tears of horror. Tears of agony. Tears of blinding, bitter madness.

This was her fate. To be punished day after day after miserably long day.

Just, she remembered as her vision darkened, as Prometheus had been punished so long ago.

CHAPTER FOUR

He couldn't stop thinking about her.

Prometheus paced the length of the library in his lonely castle, his blood humming with lust as he remembered the kiss he'd shared with Keia in the gazebo. She hadn't appeared to him in two days. Not in his dreams, not in his waking hours. Hadn't once called to him in all that time, either. He'd yet to hear her voice since she'd poofed out of his arms in the early morning light, and he was going nuts waiting for her to contact him again. Not only because he didn't like the thought of her anywhere near Zeus, but because he itched with the need to touch her. To taste her. To feel her everywhere.

This need was stronger than anything he'd ever felt. Not just lust, he knew, but something more, something primitive, something so all-consuming it was all he could focus on.

His mind skipped back over the blood he'd found in the gazebo, and his steps slowed as he remembered the way she'd abruptly left him—twice now. She'd told him the blood had been animal, not hers, but he couldn't stop wondering if they were somehow connected. She'd said she was a prisoner. He, better than anyone, knew how the king of the gods treated prisoners. He thought back to her creamy flesh in the low-cut green gown and her flawless face. She hadn't appeared hurt when she'd come to him, but she knew how to use magic, and if Zeu—

Voices sounded from the corridor, bringing his head around. His heart picked up speed when he realized one voice was female. Was it her? Was she back? He stepped toward the door, excitement burning like fire in his blood, only to draw to a stop when his daughter Natasa and her mate, Titus, appeared at the threshold of the room.

Disappointment swept through him, a disappointment he tried to mask.

"There you are," Natasa said with a smile as she crossed toward him, slid her arms around his waist, and pressed her cheek to his chest. "Hi, *pateras*."

Pateras. Father. He didn't feel much like a father. He felt like a failure when it came to her.

His arms drifted around her slim shoulders, and he hugged her back, but when he looked down and caught sight of her flame-red hair—red thanks to the fire element he'd hidden from the gods in her blood hundreds of years ago and which had caused her intense pain until she'd been reborn in the flames—the guilt he always felt around her consumed him again.

She was safe, he told himself. No longer suffering. And she was happy. His gaze drifted to Titus, standing with his hands tucked into the front pockets of his jeans, his dark wavy locks tied at his nape with a leather strap, a bemused expression across his face.

Titus loved Prometheus's daughter. Would do anything to protect her. Their bond was strong and real and deep.

His gaze drifted back down to Natasa. To her flame-red hair. Hair that was as red as Keia's.

Urgency pushed in again. He needed to find Keia. Couldn't go on waiting. Why the hell hadn't she appeared to him yet?

Natasa eased back and looked up. "We came out to invite you to dinner tonight."

His daughter was speaking to him but he could barely make out her words. All he could think about was the witch.

"*Pateras?*" she asked. Then, "Titus?"

Footsteps sounded close, followed by Titus's quiet voice. "He's blocking me. I can't tell what he's thinking." Then louder, "Prometheus? Dude, are you feeling all right? You don't look so good."

Prometheus blinked several times and finally focused on his daughter's worried face, then looked past her to her mate's narrowed hazel eyes. Titus stood behind Natasa, his hand resting on her shoulder, the ancient Greek text that marked his and all the Argonaut's forearms visible in the lamplight.

The male wasn't wearing his ever-present gloves. Titus had the ability to not only hear others' thoughts, but to pick up their emotions through touch. That ability, Prometheus knew, was one Titus had always considered a curse. But with Natasa he liked knowing what she was feeling. One look at his daughter's face told Prometheus she was feeling fear and confusion...all because of him.

That knowledge jolted him out of his trance. Fixing a relaxed look on his face—as relaxed as he could manage considering his focus remained locked on Keia—he smiled. "I'm fine. How are both of you?"

Natasa's worry fled, and she reached for her father's hand. "Good. Titus has to leave on a mission in the human realm with the Argonauts day after tomorrow so we thought we'd cook dinner for you tonight. It is your birthday, you know."

His birthday. He'd totally forgotten it was his birthday. At his age, one didn't celebrate birthdays anymore. Especially when one's life was as empty as his. A birthday was just a reminder of the passing years and the life he wasn't living. But today he wanted to celebrate. Just not with his daughter and her mate. He wanted to celebrate with Keia.

A renewed urge to find her rushed through him. To see her. To touch her and taste her. To make sure she was okay. If she wasn't going to come to him, he needed to go to her. He'd go back to the gazebo.

Find a way to contact her. There had to be something in that gazebo that could draw her back to him. He didn't know what but maybe if he used his Titan powers he could—

"*Pateras?*" Natasa said again. "You're starting to worry me."

Prometheus blinked again and looked down at his daughter. But inside, his heart was racing.

"No need to worry." Grasping Natasa at the biceps—careful not to graze Titus's fingertips in the process—Prometheus pressed a kiss to the top of her head and released her. "Thanks for the invite but I actually have plans tonight. And I'm already late so I should get going."

"You do?" Natasa's brow lowered as Prometheus stepped around her and Titus. "With whom?"

"With a female."

Surprise and approval lit Natasa's eyes as she looked up at her mate, then back at Prometheus. She knew he never made plans. "Who is she?"

Stopping at the threshold of the library, he looked back. "A witch. And before you say anything, I know what I'm doing."

"I'm sure you do. Have fun, I guess." A wry smile spread across Natasa's lips. "And don't do anything stupid."

Before he knew what he was doing, he smiled back. "I won't."

And he wouldn't. Because what he planned to do with Keia wouldn't be the least bit stupid. It would be hot and wild and, if she let him, mind-meltingly satisfying for both of them.

* * * *

She couldn't keep doing this.

The reality of Circe's situation was a heavy weight on her shoulders as she focused her powers to bring the gazebo into focus. Zeus's shade had hit her again just as her strength had returned from the attack that had pulled her away from Prometheus two days ago. She never knew when the shade was going to come, which made it impossible for her to prepare herself for his assault. If she had any hope of surviving this nightmare she needed to spend her time focusing her powers to protect herself rather than wasting them building this fantasyland.

That knowledge caused an ache to spread out from the center of her chest. Not because it meant she was going to disappoint Zeus by not getting him the element he wanted, but because it meant no longer seeing Prometheus.

She'd thought long and hard about this decision while her body had been healing. When she was stronger, when she knew how to fight the shade, then she could come back and find Prometheus again. But right now she needed to protect herself or she'd never have the strength to go through with her plan.

"Keia."

Fabric rustled behind her in the fading afternoon light. Startled out of her thoughts, Circe turned to see Prometheus rising from the chaise and striding toward her. Her pulse shot up as he drew near. His hazel eyes were a little bit wild, a whole lot hot, and when he reached her and his hand brushed her elbow, electrical impulses shot from the spot straight into her belly.

She swallowed hard, told herself to be tough. That she'd come here to say good-bye for now, not get lost in his immortal good looks and fabulous scent of pine and citrus. But her resistance wavered as he pulled her in, as his long, lean body brushed hers, and his mouth lowered to draw her into a blistering hot kiss.

His lips were just as fierce as his eyes, and the moment his tongue dipped inside to stroke against hers, all the reasons she'd told herself she couldn't have him faded in the ether.

Her hands slid up his chest and around his neck. Her breasts tingled as she leaned into him, as she kissed him back, as she melted in his arms like honey. A moan rumbled from his chest, and he tightened his arms around her, drawing her even closer to his heat and energy and life. Her fingers drifted into the silky hair at his nape. Desire turned to a frantic urge she couldn't resist. In a haze, she realized she was moving, being drawn forward as he moved back, but she didn't care. All she could focus on was his desperate kiss, his commanding hands turning her in the gazebo, the way his erection pressed against her with a heedless need of its own.

"Gods, Keia." His fingers found the line of buttons down her spine as his lips moved to her jaw. Shivers rushed over her as he breathed hot across her skin and pressed a wicked line of kisses down her throat. "I haven't been able to think about anything but you since you left."

His hands made quick work of the buttons on her dress as she trailed her fingers down his muscular back and up and under the black T-shirt he wore. Sparks of desire coiled in her belly, made her thighs tremble in anticipation. Her eyes slid closed as she traced the carved lines of his abs and savored the sensation. "Me too." Oh gods, she couldn't think when he kissed her like that. "I mean you. Titos...don't stop doing that."

A primitive growl—a sound laced with a burning passion she felt all the way to her toes—echoed from his chest. He drew a breath away, grasped the pale blue dress at her shoulders, and pushed it down her arms. Cool air washed over her breasts as he bared them to his view. Her nipples tightened, and when his eyes darkened and his approving gaze swept over her, those tingles in her belly ricocheted straight into her sex.

"I think I'm going mad, but I don't care." He palmed her right breast, lifted it in his hand as he lowered his head. "I need to taste you."

"Oh, yes..."

His tongue swept over her nipple, and she groaned and threaded her fingers back into his hair, reveling in the wicked sensations and heady desire spinning around her.

He licked and laved her nipple, sending her need into overdrive.

With his other hand, he palmed her left breast, pushed them together and teased both nipples with his tongue. Her breaths grew shallow and fast. Her sex contracted with the need to feel him everywhere. Sliding her hands back down to his shoulders, she somehow managed to find the hem of his T-shirt and pull the garment up his spine.

He drew away so she could tug the shirt off. Tossing it on the ground, she reached for him again but he moved quickly, his hands bunching in the fabric at her waist. Before she knew what was happening, he pushed the dress all the way to the floor and moaned.

"Oh, Keia..."

She was naked beneath the dress. In her haste to get here and tell him she was leaving for good, she hadn't thought to conjure undergarments. Something in the back of her mind warned this was her last chance to leave. That she needed to get out of here before this went too far. But as he lowered to his knees, her sex clenched and she knew she was lost. There was no way she could leave now. Not when he was looking at her like she was the only thing he'd ever wanted.

He coaxed her to lift one foot out of the fabric at her feet and step back. The chaise brushed against her calves. He pushed the dress aside, inched forward on his knees, and grasped her hand in his, pulling her down to sit.

"Turn, Keia." His hands landed on her knees, pushing her legs apart. As she turned slightly, he slid one hand under the back of her knee and lifted her foot to the seat. Her spine pressed into the plush cushions as he positioned her. Then he was moving closer, his hands trailing up the insides of her thighs, his hot breath fanning her sex until she was trembling with need.

He parted her with his fingers, stared down at her as if she were a feast he couldn't wait to devour. Her stomach quivered with anticipation. Her hands shook against the seat of the chaise. When he didn't make a move, she knew she couldn't wait any longer. On a desperate breath, she reached for him, wrapped her hand around the back of his head, and pulled him closer. "Taste me, Titos. Don't make me wait."

"Yes," he breathed against her. Then his tongue swept over her clit, sending shards of pleasure all through her core.

She moaned. Lifted her hips to his wicked touch. Shivered as he circled her clit then trailed his tongue down to her opening and pressed inside.

Her eyes slid closed as she leaned back. All she knew was his touch, his tongue moving against her to drive her mad, his hands sliding up her belly to cup and tease her breasts. Heat prickled her skin, made her need that much hotter. She lifted and lowered her hips in time with his frantic strokes, moving faster as the orgasm built. And when he drew her over-sensitized nub between his lips and suckled, the wave of ecstasy broke over her like a tidal wave cresting the mountains.

She cried out, trembled against his lips as the pleasure raced along her nerve endings. The wave slowly faded, and vaguely she became aware of her surroundings, of the darkness pressing in from outside the gazebo, of the soft cushion beneath her, of her knees open, one leaning against the back of the chaise. But then his lips moved over her hip, her belly, trailing a line of hot kisses up to her breasts, and she forgot about everything but him.

Her hands found his shoulders. Her fingers pressed against his strong muscles. She lifted her head, grasped him and pulled, forcing him up from the floor. Finding his mouth with hers, she kissed him with everything she had in her, wanting to give him exactly what he'd given her. Wanting him to know pleasure like nothing he'd ever known.

He groaned into her mouth as he rose over her. Her hands slid down to the waistband of his jeans while she flicked her tongue against his and sat upright. Finding the button, she popped it free then slipped her hands beneath the fabric and pushed it down his hips.

He kissed her harder. One hand moved to the back of the chaise, the other slid into her hair to tip her head so he could kiss her deeper. As she worked the fabric down his rock hard thighs and past his knees, he moved closer, rested one leg on the seat of the chaise so she could tug the garment free and throw it on the ground, kissing her the whole time as if he couldn't get enough.

Need resurged within her as she drew her hands up the backs of his thighs, over the soft layer of hair on his legs, then around to his front. Licking into his mouth, she closed one hand around the base of his cock. He groaned again. His fingertips dug into her skull. Sliding her hand up the thick cylinder of flesh, she cuffed the end and squeezed. A bead of fluid slid from the tip, making her mouth water. With her thumb, she spread it over the sensitive underside of the head and drew her hand down and back up.

He drew back from her mouth. Pulsed in her fist. "You make me weak," he rasped. Letting go of the back of the chaise, he trailed the pad of his thumb along her wet, bottom lip. "I want to feel these lips around my cock."

"Oh yes..." She grew wet and hot and achy with his words. Her hand shifted up to his ass, and she pulled him closer, forcing him higher above her as she angled forward and drew his cock toward her.

She breathed hot over his erection, watched it twitch. He trembled as she flicked her tongue against the tip and squeezed the base, teasing him with the lightest of touches.

"More," he growled, shifting closer. A vein pulsed in his neck. His face flushed with arousal. "Taste me. Suck me, Keia."

She groaned as she looked up at him. And when his hand drifted to the back of her head, she finally closed her mouth over his length and sucked.

He groaned long and deep. Pushed forward with his hips until he breached her throat, then drew back. Licking the underside every time the tip passed over her tongue, Circe pleasured him with her mouth, wanting him to find the same release he'd given her, wanting to give him everything. He grew harder with every suck, with every lick, with every press and glide and retreat.

"Yes, Keia." His fingertips tightened in her hair. "Don't stop."

She didn't. Flicking faster with her tongue, she sucked deeper as his thrusts picked up speed. Her other hand found his balls and squeezed. She did it again and again, until she felt his cock begin to swell. And when she sensed he was on the edge, when she felt his climax about to peak, she drew him all the way in and swallowed around his sensitive head.

His pleasure erupted into her mouth. A long, guttural groan echoed from his chest. His fingertips dug into her skull as he thrust once, twice, three more times and trembled.

She continued to work him with her mouth, swallowing every drop, bringing him down slowly. His hips angled back long seconds later, releasing him from her lips. Breathing deeply, she swiped the back of her hand over her mouth and looked up with a smile of satisfaction, of pride, of her own pleasure that she'd been able to give him what he'd given her.

He moved quickly, sweeping his arms around her, lifting her from the chaise. Her smile morphed to a gasp. In a rush, he slid beneath her, and before she realized what was happening she was straddling his hips and his mouth was beneath hers, drawing her right back into a kiss that was so blisteringly hot, lust resurged within her.

He tugged her down and devoured her mouth. His rock hard erection slid through her wetness, reminding her he was a Titan. He could go for days without growing soft if he wanted. A fact that now sent a shiver of excitement down her spine.

"Take me," he mouthed against her, lifting his hips until he pressed against her opening. "Ride me. Use me. Fuck me. Now."

She couldn't say no because that was all she wanted now too. Grasping the back of the chaise, she lowered her weight. Her tongue swept into his mouth just as his cock pressed into her core. Groaning, she tightened around his length until he was seated so far inside they became one.

"Oh, fuck, yes." His hands landed against her hips. He used them to help her lift and lower. Flexed his hips so he drove in deeper. Against her mouth he groaned and kissed her again. Pleasure arced all through her body as she rode him, as their passions grew together, as he pressed into her with long, deep, blinding thrusts.

A frenzied high the likes of which she'd never known hovered just out of her reach. She moved faster. Kissed him harder. Needed to reach it. Needed to drag him into the abyss with her. Needed everything. Sweat beaded her skin, melded with his. She groaned, lifted, lowered, trembled as he hit that perfect spot again and again. Pulling her mouth from his, she dropped her head back and gave herself over to the moment, to every touch, to the way it pushed her right to the edge.

"Come for me, Keia." His hot breath washed over her neck. One hand closed around her breast, and then his mouth was there, suckling her nipple. Shards of ecstasy shot from her breast into her sex. Light blinded her. She cried out. And as the orgasm consumed her, she realized the pleasure she felt with him was better than anything she'd ever felt, not because he was a Titan or even a god, but because he was the first person in ages that mattered.

Slowly, she became aware of the gazebo once more. Candles she didn't remember lighting blazed around them. Somehow she'd ended up on her back on the chaise with Prometheus's heavy weight pressing into her from above, his sweat-slicked skin plastered to hers. She didn't remember him flipping her, didn't remember much of anything besides the most delicious orgasm of her life.

"Holy Hades, witch," he breathed against her neck. "You totally wrecked me."

No, he'd wrecked her. More than she'd thought possible. Nerves echoed through her belly and chest, a feeling she didn't understand. What was happening to her? Was she falling for him? She wasn't supposed to fall for him. She was supposed to use him. And if she couldn't stomach using him, she was supposed to walk away. But right now she didn't want to walk away. She just wanted a repeat of the wicked pleasure he'd given her only moments ago.

Her throat grew thick as she looked up at the shadows dancing over the ceiling from the candles, so similar to the shadows she watched on the ceiling of her cell as she lay on her measly blanket when the flames in her cauldron died out. A bitter reality circled around her.

Nothing had changed.

No, that wasn't right. Her chest pinched. Something had definitely changed.

Her heart had changed.

No matter how badly she wanted to be free, she wouldn't risk him. Not now, not when she knew she was falling for him. If she told him the truth about her imprisonment—now or when she'd learned to fight the shade—she had a feeling he'd come after her. He might succeed in freeing her from Zeus's hell by doing so, but he'd put himself at risk. Zeus had a long memory. Yes, the king of the gods wanted the water element in his quest for ultimate power, but he would also love to see Prometheus suffer once more. And nothing would make Prometheus suffer more than being chained all over again.

She couldn't let that happen. Which meant she wasn't just going to walk away for now. To save him, she needed to walk away forever.

Something hot burned behind her eyes. Something she wasn't used to. She blinked several times, knowing more than anything that she just wanted to go on lying there in his arms, but couldn't.

She shifted beneath him. Taking her hint, he rolled to his side on the chaise, propped his elbow on the cushion and his head on his hand, and smiled down at her. "That was amazing." His hand drifted from her shoulder, across her collarbone, and down the center of her chest, right between her breasts, sending tingles over her skin. "I love this body. And I plan to have it each and every way tonight before you have to leave."

Her eyes slid closed as his warm hand drifted lower, over her belly button and down her lower abs. Gods, that was all she wanted too, but she knew if he started that wicked plan, she'd never have the strength to leave.

Capturing his hand before it could slide between her legs, she lifted it to her mouth and kissed his palm. And then, pushing up so she was sitting, she moved his hand to his naked hip, pinned it there, and leaned in to feather a kiss against his luscious mouth. "I wish I had time for that, but I don't."

She rose, found her gown on the floor, and pulled it on.

"You have to go already?" Confusion drew his brows together as he sat up. "But you just got here. I haven't seen you in days."

"I know." She reached back and buttoned her dress, turning away so she wouldn't have to see the disappointment in his hazel eyes. "And I'm sorry. Believe me. If I could stay, I would."

"Keia."

The floor creaked behind her. His hands landed on her shoulders, turning her to face him. "I want more than these brief visits. I was sort of hoping you wanted more too."

Her heart squeezed tight as she looked up at him. She did want more. She wanted everything. But that wasn't her future, and she had no one to blame for this gigantic mess but herself. "Titos, this is the last time I'm going to visit you."

Panic widened his eyes, and his fingers tightened around her shoulders. "What?"

She pushed back the pain, unwilling to let it consume her. When she was alone in her cell again, then she'd wallow in it. But now she needed to be strong. For him, but mostly for her. "I can't keep coming here. It's not fair to either of us. It's too draining on my powers, and as you said, it's disrupting your life."

"Since meeting you, I finally have a life." His intense gaze swept over her features. "Tell me where you are. I'll come find you."

The pain she'd tried to fight back lanced her chest. His declaration was exactly what she'd wanted when she'd hatched this crazy plan, but now there was no way she could let it happen. "You can't."

"Yes, I can. I'm a Titan. Tell me where you are. I'm not afraid of Zeus."

"I know you're not," she whispered, lifting to her toes and pressing her lips against his for one last kiss. "But I am." She lowered to her heels as tears filled her eyes. Tears that were as foreign to her as this heaviness in her chest. "I'm sorry, Prometheus. I'm sorry for everything."

Before she could change her mind, she cut the feed. The dank rock walls of her cell replaced the gazebo's ornate columns. Prometheus's frantic, "Come back," echoed in her ears as the agony of loss settled deep into her bones. And in a moment of clarity she knew the shade wasn't the greatest threat to her life.

Caring for someone else—caring for Prometheus and never seeing him again—would decimate her far worse than that monster ever could.

CHAPTER FIVE

The last time...

Prometheus stood in the middle of the gazebo long minutes after Keia disappeared. Something had happened to spook her. Something over the last two days when she'd been away. He'd been so obsessed with touching her—with having her—that he hadn't picked up on her signals when she'd finally appeared.

The dream—or had it been a vision?—which he'd had days ago, drifted through his mind. He had the gift of foresight. He could see alternate futures. But those futures were often hazy when they involved himself. This one had been clear, though: Zeus, controlling her, leading him to his death. Only he was a Titan. He couldn't be killed. Not by conventional means. He could be captured, though.

A warning tingle rushed down his spine as he turned a slow circle, looking over the gazebo in the early evening light but seeing none of it. Was she a plant by Zeus? Was this a trick to lure him to imprisonment once more? He didn't want to believe it but she herself had said she'd made a deal with the king of the gods. He'd been so obsessed with her he hadn't pushed that issue when he'd seen her last. Then he'd gotten lost in her sweet, seductive kiss.

Her words—before she'd been pulled away the last time—echoed in his mind: *"You're the only thing I have to look forward to, Titos. I know it's not fair to you, but I think about you all the time. Even when I shouldn't."* Followed by the memory of that blood and the blinding pain he'd felt when he'd touched it.

His heart sped up, beating a bruising rhythm against his ribs. None of that could be a trick. He'd felt the desperation in her kiss, heard the truth in her words, and the blood...she'd said it was animal, but he knew in his gut it had been her blood. He wasn't sure how he knew, he just did. And the pain he'd felt when he'd touched it had been hers as well.

She was in danger. She was with Zeus, in some kind of cave, he remembered her saying at one point, and she was in danger of—

"Holy shit." His eyes flew wide. He'd heard his daughter and Titus speak of one witch who lived high in the caves of Mt. Olympus. One who'd helped the Argonauts not long ago. Only she didn't go by the name Keia.

He pictured the Argolean castle in the heart of the capital city of Tiyrns and teleported into the foyer of the marble structure. As a god, he had the power to flash through walls, something the Argolean people could not do. The guards stationed at the main doors turned at the sound of his appearance. Their eyes grew wide as they drew their swords. In seconds they were rushing toward him.

He didn't have time for this nonsense. Wanted nothing more than to backhand the guards into next week. The only thing that kept him from doing so was the fact his daughter was invested in this realm and that he didn't want to make things worse for her.

Six guards surrounded him, swords and spears drawn and pointed right at his heart. Holding up his hands in a nonthreatening way, Prometheus said, "I want no trouble. I've just come to find the Argonaut Aristokles."

The guards didn't back down. Voices echoed in the three-story entry. Just when Prometheus's patience was about to hit its limit, he heard Titus's voice from the balcony above.

"What in Hades?" Titus rushed down the wide, curved staircase, waving the guards back with his hand. "He's with me. He's fine. Let him through."

The guards slowly lowered their weapons and stood at attention. Titus drew close, his hair pulled back, his hands covered in those ever-present gloves, a look of bewilderment across his weathered face. "What's going on? Why are you here?" Panic rushed across his features. "Natasa isn't—"

"No," Prometheus said quickly, recognizing that quick shot of fear in Titus's eyes...the same fear he was feeling for Keia. "I'm not here about Natasa. I haven't even seen her. I need to speak with Aristokles."

"Ari?" Titus's brow wrinkled. "He's not here. He's in the human realm. On a scouting mission."

Shit. "Where?"

"I don't know. He hasn't checked in since last night."

Frustration pummeled Prometheus from every side. "What about the princess?"

"Elysia?"

That was her name. He was so far removed from the politics of this realm, he barely paid attention to who was related to whom. "Yes. Where is she?"

"In a meeting with the queen and the Council. Prometheus, what's this about?"

Prometheus swiped a hand against his suddenly sweaty brow. "It's about Olympus. I need to know what Aristokles and the princess saw when they went to Mt. Olympus."

"To rescue Cerek?"

"Yes."

"Why?"

Holy Hades. Prometheus liked Titus for the most part, but right now he was ready to shake some sense into the Argonaut. "Because someone's life might be in danger thanks to that rescue."

Titus clearly didn't understand, and Prometheus was past the point of wanting to explain. "Where's Cerek? Is he here?"

"Yeah, he's in the training center with Max."

Prometheus turned on his heels. "Maybe he can help me."

The training center was a domed structure on the castle grounds. It consisted of a gym, weight room, medical facility, and classrooms. Searching rooms, Prometheus finally located Cerek in a medical bay having his shoulder stitched up by a healer.

Prometheus didn't bother to wait until the Argonaut was done, just stalked into the room without waiting for an invitation. The healer glanced over with an annoyed look. Cerek, shirtless and seated on an exam table, looked up as he and Titus entered. "Hey," he said as the healer placed a bandage on his arm. "What's up with you two?"

"What happened?" Titus asked, nodding toward Cerek's arm.

"Nothing. Just took my eyes off Max when I shouldn't have."

Max was an Argonaut in training, Prometheus remembered from a conversation with his daughter. Young. Cocky. A little bit reckless. He'd spent time in the Underworld as a kid. That had to fuck a person up.

"Where is he now?" Titus asked.

"With Zander. Probably getting a lecture about taking it easy on the old folks."

Titus nodded. The healer said, "You're done. Just keep this dry for a few hours so it has time to heal."

"Thanks." Climbing off the table as the healer left the room, Cerek reached for his shirt. "So what's going on?"

"That's what I'd like to know," Titus muttered.

Prometheus's jaw clenched. "Aristokles and the princess mentioned a witch on Olympus when they went to rescue you. I need to know why she's there."

Cerek glanced at Titus and back to Prometheus with a perplexed expression. "She's there because she works for Zeus. She's the one who reprogrammed me."

Zeus's Sirens had shot Cerek with a poisoned arrow twenty-five years ago. The Argonauts had all thought he'd died, but the poison had preserved his body in stone. Zeus had taken him to Olympus and wiped his memory so he didn't know who he was or where he'd come from. He'd only recently regained his memory when he'd been rescued by the princess and the Argonauts. "In a cave?"

"Yeah." The wrinkle in Cerek's brow deepened. "On Mt. Olympus. Why?"

Prometheus's conversation with Keia days ago ran through his memory.

"What does he want from you?"

"He wants to punish me."

"Why?"

"Because I helped someone. Someone Zeus was using so he could gain more power."

"What was her name?" he asked.

Cerek frowned as if it were common knowledge. "Circe."

Circe was the daughter of Hecate, the goddess of witchcraft and the strongest sorceress to ever walk the earth. She'd never been as powerful as her mother, but Prometheus knew from his interactions with the immortal world before his imprisonment that the daughter of Hecate had craved power as much as Zeus himself.

Keia. Goddess pharmakeia. That's what the commoners had called Circe for years. His eyes widened with understanding. She'd told him who she was with that name, and he still hadn't clued in because he'd been so obsessed with her.

"Find me, Titos..."

She worked for Zeus. She'd sought him out, appeared to him, seduced him so the king of the gods could recapture him. And he'd fallen for it. Even told her he'd risk facing Zeus to find her.

"Why the sudden interest in Circe?" Cerek asked. "Is she in danger?"

Prometheus turned away, his heart pounding hard with both adrenaline and utter stupidity. No, the witch wasn't in danger. He was.

"I don't know," Titus muttered. "But there's clearly something going on. And before you ask, no I can't read him."

Silence stretched over the room as Prometheus thought back over every interaction he'd had with the witch.

"Elysia's had nothing but regret about leaving Circe in that cave," Cerek said long seconds later. "She didn't have to help us, but she did. I guarantee Zeus has come up with some twisted form of punishment for her because of us. He keeps all kinds of sick monsters trapped in the bowels of Mt. Olympus."

The memory of that blood hit Prometheus again. He turned to look back at the Argonauts. "What did you just say?"

Cerek met his gaze. "I said Zeus is probably punishing her because of us. That witch is as much a prisoner as I ever was."

As much as Prometheus ever was.

"I was not always a good witch, Titos. But I want to be one. I hope you believe that."

He'd felt the truth in those words when she'd said them, did believe them even if she'd kept her identity secret, and every time he though about that blood, each time he remembered the agony he'd felt when he'd touched it, he knew Cerek was right. She was being punished for helping the Argonauts. And judging by the way she'd been pulled away from Prometheus during the times they'd been together, that punishment had happened right before his eyes, and he hadn't realized it.

He'd been punished daily by Zeus. Chained to a rock in the blistering heat of the sun, unable to move as he waited for a giant eagle to slice into his side with its razor sharp beak, rip out his liver, and leave him in blinding pain until the wounds slowly closed and consciousness returned.

Yes, Zeus could come up with all kinds of horrendous punishments. For a witch who'd helped the Argonauts, Prometheus knew the king of the gods would not hold back.

The urge to find her, to save her, to rescue her from the same kind of hell he'd lived through overwhelmed Prometheus. "You're certain she's on Mt. Olympus."

"Yeah," Cerek answered. "She can't leave there. Her magic's confined to the mountain."

"Where? Where is her cave?"

"At the top. There's a path that winds all the way up."

Prometheus's mind spun. He could transport to Olympus. The minute he stepped foot into the realm of the heavens, though, Zeus would know. The king of the gods would sense him. He wouldn't have much time to find Circe and transport her to freedom.

"Thank you." Plans ricocheted through Prometheus's brain as he turned away from the Argonauts.

He made it two steps before his daughter's mate stepped in his path and held up both gloved hands. "Hold up. You're not thinking about going to Olympus to get her, are you?"

"No, I'm not thinking about it." He'd already decided.

Titus's jaw tightened. "You're walking into a trap. You know that, don't you? All for a witch."

He might be, but he didn't care. Witch or not, Circe made him feel alive in a way nothing and no one had in over a thousand years. Regardless of why she'd sought him out—whether it was her doing or Zeus's—he wouldn't leave her to the same torment he'd endured.

Before Titus could stop him, he pictured Zeus's precious mountain and flashed.

* * * *

Mt. Olympus was cold and dark when he arrived.

The sun had set. Night pressed in from all sides as Prometheus stood behind a rock outcropping, staring toward a dark cave opening. There had to be more than a hundred caves on this damn mountain, but he'd yet to pass a single one. This had to be the right place.

He hoped it was, at least, because Zeus had probably already been alerted to an outside force in his realm. It wouldn't take long for the king of the gods to zero in on that energy and locate Prometheus.

"You'd better be there," Prometheus whispered beneath the starry sky.

He moved away from his shelter and into the tunnel. Cool air washed over his cheeks, sending a shiver down his spine. It was dark, but his Titan eyesight picked out every bump and ridge on the rock walls. He followed the tunnel around twists and curves until it opened to a vast room with a raised platform and a pedestal topped with a copper bowl. No sound echoed from the space. No movement to cut the silence. He climbed the steps and circled the bowl, recognizing it as a cauldron. Circe's, he guessed.

He lifted his gaze and scanned the room. Two arched doorways opened off the space. Moving in that direction, he peeked into a bedchamber and another room that housed rows and rows of books, a small sitting area, and a basic kitchen.

This was where she lived. Where Zeus had trapped her for over a thousand years to conjure her spells under his bidding. But she wasn't here now. His heart pounded hard as he rationalized where she could be.

Cerek had said she was confined to this mountain. That because of Zeus's curse she couldn't leave. She had to be here. He hadn't seen any other cave openings when he'd wandered up the path. That didn't mean they weren't out there but—

His mind shot back to the moment he'd stepped into the tunnel and the burst of cool air that had washed over his face.

It had come from the left. There'd been another tunnel.

He rushed back to the opening, found the second tunnel and realized why he'd missed it. It curved at a right angle, leaving the appearance of nothing but rock. Moving around the corner, he followed the second tunnel down as it wound deep into the center of Mt. Olympus.

The air was colder down here. Musty. Water dripped along the rock walls, puddled over the ground. He placed a hand on the cool stones as he followed the path, scanning the tunnel for changes, for threats, for Zeus himself.

The tunnel widened to a central, circular space. Several doors made of metal bars lined the room. One was dark and empty, opening to another tunnel that led deeper into the bowels of the mountain. His gaze skipped back to the doors. Cell doors, he realized. The trickle of liquid running under one drew his attention. He stepped toward it. Looked down. Realized the liquid wasn't water, but blood.

"Circe?" Panic tightened into a fist around his throat. He grasped the bars and pulled. The door swung open easily, creaking on its hinges.

A groan echoed from inside.

Prometheus's gaze sharpened, and he spotted a shadow on the floor against the far wall. "Keia?"

The shadow shifted, and another groan echoed. Blood trickled through the rocks along the floor. In a terror-filled heartbeat, Prometheus knew it was her.

He rushed to her side, knelt, and gently turned her away from the wall where she lay curled. She cried out in pain. "I'm sorry," he whispered. "I didn't mean to—"

Blood covered his hands in the dark. As she turned onto her back and whimpered, he saw the giant gash in her neck, still spilling blood.

"Hold still." Heart racing, he placed a hand over the wound at her neck. "This may hurt, but I promise it will help."

He closed his eyes, called on his gifts. As a Titan, he had the ability to heal. It was how he'd survived that giant eagle's attack each day. He could transfer that ability to another if he focused, but this particular gift wasn't always reliable, as he didn't often use it anymore.

Who the hell was he kidding? He never used it because he isolated himself from others in that castle high in the Argolean mountains.

"Hold on," he whispered, focusing harder. Warmth gathered in his palm, permeated her skin. A golden glow radiated from where he touched her, the power of regeneration fusing her skin back together. Sweat beaded his brow. His muscles grew taut and rigid. What should already be healed wasn't. He could feel the cells binding beneath his fingers, but it was taking much too long. Something was slowing him down. Something—

"Adamant," Circe rasped, as if reading his mind. He opened his eyes to focus on her pain-filled face. Blood matted her hair and stained her white dress. "This cell is lined...with adamant. He drags me in here to keep me from casting...a spell to stop him."

His gaze shot up to the rocks. Adamant was the strongest ore in all the realms. It didn't just block her spells, it was weakening his gift, keeping him from healing her.

A clicking sound echoed from beyond the open door. His gaze shot in that direction. Beneath his hand, Circe stiffened.

"It's him," she said in a shaky voice, one filled not just with fear but with terror. "He's come back. He's early. You have to leave. You have to go before—"

A low snarl sounded from the doorway, followed by a growl that was both man and beast at the same time. "The witch is my prize. Back away."

Prometheus let go of Circe and slowly pushed to his feet. She reached out, trying to stop him, but she was so weak from the blood loss, her fingers grazed his arm and dropped away. Focusing his eyesight, Prometheus zeroed in on the monster only to realize it was human.

No, not totally human. Part of it reeked of death. It was a shade. A death shadow that preyed on blood. It had attacked her. Continued to attack her, Prometheus realized when he remembered the way she'd been abruptly drawn away from him several times.

"Leave her or there will be consequences," Prometheus said to the shade. A promise, not a warning.

The shade moved into the room, its long nails clicking an ominous sound against the floor. "And who will provide them? You? Your powers are useless down here, god. Adamant doesn't affect the dead, but it does the living."

"Titos," Circe called in a frantic voice.

"Then it's a good thing I'm not just any god. I'm a Titan."

The shade's eyes widened, then it snarled and lunged.

CHAPTER SIX

The shade knocked Prometheus back into the rocks. His head hit the wall with a crack. Near his feet, Circe shrieked.

The shade was strong from drinking the witch's blood. Prometheus, on the other hand, was weakened thanks to the adamant in the walls around him. Grasping the shade at the shoulders, he managed to keep the beast from ripping into the flesh of his arms and shoved the monster back.

His Titan strength may be weakened, but that didn't mean he still wasn't stronger than this piece of shit.

The shade hit the far wall, bounced off, growled, and charged again. Prometheus waited until it drew close, then captured it by the waist, whipped around as he lifted it off its feet, and slammed it to the ground.

The shade whimpered but struggled under Prometheus's hold.

"The only way...to kill a shade," Circe managed from the corner of the room, "is to pierce its heart."

Pierce its heart. That clearly could only be done when it was in human form. Which meant Prometheus had to work fast before it used up Circe's blood reserved and morphed back into a death shadow. Which it was doing quickly as it exerted its strength to fight.

Pressing his weight into the shade to hold him still, Prometheus scanned the room for anything he could use to stake the fucker. The room was empty except for a wooden chair in the opposite corner from where Circe sat.

Dragging the struggling shade with him, Prometheus shoved the shade against the wall with one hand, held it tight by the throat, and broke a leg free of the chair with the other.

The shade snapped and snarled as the rest of the chair fell into a pile of wood against the floor. "What do you think you're going to do with that? You can't kill me. I'm already dead."

"You're right. I can't kill you. But I can send you to Hades once and for all for what you've done." He jammed the chair leg straight through the shade's heart.

The shade's eyes went bug wide, then its entire body disintegrated into ash and fluttered to the floor.

The stake crashed against the ground. Coughing, Prometheus fanned the ash away from his face and quickly moved back to Circe's side.

"Careful," he said when she reached for his arm. "You're still bleeding." Placing his hand back over the wound in her neck, he focused his gift so the tissue could begin to heal.

"You're not safe here," she rasped. "You have to go."

"Shh." He wrapped his arm around her and held her while he let his gift work. "Don't move too much just yet."

She stopped trying to turn and sank into him. "How did you find me?"

"The Argonauts." When her brow wrinkled, he added, "Cerek."

"But how did you know who I was?"

"I finally used my superhuman brain." Her frown deepened in such an adorable way, he chuckled. "Okay, it's not so superhuman. I just put your clues together. Keia. Goddess pharmakeia. I remembered that was what the commoners used to call the witch Circe. And when I thought back to what you'd said about Zeus punishing you for helping another, I realized you were the witch who helped rescue Cerek from Zeus's service."

Her green eyes softened in the dark. "I'm sorry," she whispered. "I wanted to tell you who I was, but I couldn't. There are rules."

"I know." He lifted his hand, checked the wound beneath. The bleeding had stopped. The wound was still fresh, but a layer of new skin was already beginning to form. "And I'm not upset. I understand why you couldn't tell me." His gaze drifted to her face. "Though you should have told me about that shade."

Tears filled her eyes. "I wanted to, but I couldn't. I couldn't put you in danger."

"I'm a Titan, Circe. Even weakened by adamant, I can kick a shade's ass."

"I see that. But it's not the shade I'm worried about."

Zeus. She was talking about Zeus. "He can't hurt us anymore."

"Titos—"

"Come on." He pulled her to her feet. "We need to get back up to the surface so we can get the hell out of this realm. There's not enough adamant in these walls to immobilize me, but there is enough to prevent me from teleporting."

She pushed a hand against his chest, her feet shuffling over the ground as he maneuvered her toward the door. "You don't understand. It's not the adamant keeping me here. It's—"

"It's her love of power," Zeus said from the doorway.

Prometheus drew to a stop, his arm around Circe's waist. Against him, Circe froze and whispered, "Oh gods."

"Stay behind me," Prometheus said in a low voice, pushing her back.

"There's no need for that, Titan." Zeus stepped into the room. "We're all friends here, right, witch?"

Behind Zeus, five Sirens rushed in, bows drawn, arrows poised at

Prometheus's heart.

"Just so we're clear," Zeus said. "Those arrows are made from adamant. So if you decide to bolt, Titan, you won't get far."

Prometheus's jaw tightened. His dream had become a reality, the alternate future he'd ignored. He was trapped. Again. Only this time it wasn't just him. "Let the witch go. You used her as bait and it worked. She means nothing to you and we both know it."

"Oh, she was bait," Zeus answered, lacing his fingers together behind his back. "But willing bait."

"Titos," Circe whispered in a pained voice at his back.

"Go on." Zeus lifted a hand toward the witch. "Ask her yourself. Ask her about our deal. Her freedom from this mountain in exchange for seducing you into giving her the water element."

Shock rippled through Prometheus as he turned and stared into Circe's green eyes. "Is that true?"

Guilt rushed over her flawless features. "Yes, at first. But that was before I knew you. You have to believe me. I changed my mind."

The pain of betrayal lanced his chest, as swift and sharp as that eagle's beak had ever been. He turned away from her.

"Never trust a female, Titan." Zeus clucked his tongue. "I thought you would have picked up that tidbit over your long lifetime."

Anger and betrayal and stupidity swam in Prometheus's veins. "When would I have picked that up? When I was chained to that rock?"

Zeus grinned. "It was a nice rock. You miss it, don't you?"

Prometheus's vision turned red. An image flashed in his mind, his hands wrapping around Zeus's throat, his arms ripping the god's head from his body and flinging it at his precious Sirens. But he'd never do that no matter how much he wanted to. Because attacking Zeus would guarantee the witch would never be freed. And even though she'd betrayed him, he still didn't want her to suffer the way he had. Wouldn't wish that kind of torment on anyone.

Anyone but Zeus, that was.

"Well, this has all been fun, but it's time to get on with things." Zeus sighed. "Sirens, take him."

"Wait." Circe jerked in front of Prometheus. "Take me instead. He told me where the water element is. You don't need him anymore. Take me."

Prometheus's gaze darted to the back of her head as the Sirens moved up behind him and tugged his arms behind his back, cuffing him with the adamant shackles that would severely limit his powers. He'd never told her where the water element was located. They'd never even discussed the water element.

"Did you really think this was about the water element?" Zeus lifted his brow in amusement. "He doesn't even know where the thing is. He scattered those elements over the earth on purpose so he'd never be able to tell another god where they're located. I know that." He angled his chin Prometheus's direction. "He knows that. You, witch, are the only one who was stupid enough to fall for that ruse."

A gasp rushed out of Circe's mouth. Zeus turned away, but she rushed after him. "I can get you what you want. I can use the chain. Access his god essence in the metal and look back into his past with my powers to see where he scattered the elements. You don't need him. You have me."

Zeus whipped back to her so fast she stumbled, then his hand closed around Circe's injured throat like a vise, and in one swift move he lifted her off the floor. Her face turned red. Her eyes bulged as she struggled to pry his hands free to no avail. Prometheus's muscles flexed and he shifted an inch forward, but the adamant cuffs held him in place. And the Sirens' daggers suddenly pushing against his side kept him from trying. "I'll always have you, witch. You think you're getting out of this cave? You're never doing anything but what I say."

He shoved her back into the wall and released her. Gasping, she fell to the floor and lifted a hand to her injured throat.

"Bring him," Zeus said to the Sirens, turning for the tunnel.

The Sirens pushed Prometheus forward. His gaze shot to Circe on the ground, tears streaming down her cheeks.

"I'm sorry," she whispered. "I'm so sorry."

Before he could answer, Zeus barked, "And bring her, too. She can watch as my new eagle feasts on the Titan's flesh."

* * * *

Circe watched in horror as the Sirens shackled Prometheus vertically to a flat rock, his arms outstretched above his head, his feet together against the ground. They were somewhere in the human realm, though she didn't know where. The landscape was dry and barren, the hills around them littered with rock outcroppings baking in the sun.

She tried again to move her arms, but her hands were cuffed together at her back with a length of adamant chain, preventing any kind of movement. She couldn't conjure a spell without her hands. Couldn't even contact Prometheus's daughter in the Argolean realm and tell her where her father was trapped. Finally, she was free from that cave, with all the power in the world within her grasp, yet she was unable to access it and save the male who'd come to mean more to her than any other.

"You know," Zeus said in a cheerful voice as the Sirens checked Prometheus's chains one last time to make sure he couldn't move. "When Circe and I hatched this plan to lure you out of hiding, Titan, I had no idea it was going to be quite so easy." Brushing a lock of hair away from Circe's cheek, Zeus smiled down at her almost sweetly.

Sickness brewed in Circe's stomach at the lies he was telling. Lies Prometheus was believing.

"She really is a find, isn't she?" Zeus went on. "As seductive as any Siren, but as cunning and manipulative as the gods. Any male would be lucky to have her on his side. And I will have her on my side." His eyes darkened with a heat that made her skin crawl. "And on her back, and on her hands and knees, all too soon. Finally, witch, you're going to submit to me the way you should have submitted long ago."

"I never agreed to this." Rage simmered along Circe's nerve endings, but she didn't pull away from Zeus's touch. Knew she wouldn't be able to even if she tried. "And I'll never submit to you. Not willingly."

"Oh, you will." Zeus's grin faded, and he dropped his hand. "Because I have your lover, and if you don't do exactly what I want this time, I'll make his torture that much worse. Do you think I'm clueless? I knew all about your plan to double cross me and have Prometheus rescue you. I even knew when you gave up that plan and decided to sacrifice yourself to that shade so selflessly in a lame attempt to spare his life. I'm the god of the heavens, witch. I know everything. I let you think you were in control. And do you know why?" His eyes narrowed on Circe as he pointed toward Prometheus. "Because his suffering is going to be that much more satisfying when that eagle's ripping into his flesh and he's thinking about all the ways I'm fucking the female who's fallen in love with him."

In love with him? Was she? Panic rushed through Circe's chest but turned to a warm liquid feeling that gave her strength.

Yes, she was in love with him. Quickly, madly, deeply in love with a Titan.

Zeus turned back to Prometheus with a smug grin. Circe's gaze followed and rested on the Titan, chained to the rock wall, and bile slid up her throat at what Zeus had planned. But Prometheus's hazel eyes weren't on Zeus. They were locked on her. And they no longer brimmed with betrayal. They swam in a sea of regret and sorrow and pain.

I'm sorry, she mouthed to him, tears filling her eyes. Did he feel any of what she did? She'd never know. Not when she was Zeus's prisoner on Olympus and he was trapped here.

Prometheus shook his head slightly, telling her in one brief motion that it wasn't her fault, that he didn't blame her, that he was sorry too.

That he *did* feel at least some of what she did.

The pain in her heart grew exponentially until it choked her throat.

"Where the hell is that eagle," Zeus said, his voice growing impatient as he glanced past Prometheus toward a dark cave opening Circe had tried—and failed—to ignore.

Almost as if on cue, a screech echoed from inside the cave.

"That's more like it." Zeus grinned down at Circe once more. "Let's get this show on the road so we can get on to other, more enjoyable activities."

Sickness threatened to overwhelm Circe, but she kept her gaze locked on Prometheus. Refused to give Zeus even a fraction of her concentration. Wanted him to know that she wouldn't leave him until forced.

Light flashed to her left. Zeus muttered a curse and turned in that direction. Voices echoed—several, male—dragging at Circe's attention. She finally looked that way, eyes widening when she spotted two, three, no seven Argonauts, their arms and hands covered in the ancient Greek text of their forefathers as they drew their swords and rushed toward Prometheus.

"Stop them!" Zeus screamed. Lifting his hand toward the heavens, he grasped a lightning bolt out of thin air and hurled it toward the Argonauts.

The six Sirens who'd accompanied them to this place abandoned Prometheus and reached for their bows, readying for battle. The Argonauts jumped out of the way of Zeus's lightning bolt and continued streaking toward them. Shock widened each of the Sirens' eyes. Only one was able to grasp her bow in time. The others quickly reached for their secondary weapons, the daggers strapped to their thighs.

Zeus continued hurling lighting bolts, barely missing one of his

Sirens. The Argonauts darted away from his bolts, rolled across the ground to avoid being singed. Argonaut clashed with Siren, the sound of a battle rising in the air. Unable to move, to do anything to help, Circe looked back at Prometheus and spotted a flash of red out of the corner of her eye, rushing his way.

Seconds later the entire rock outcropping was engulfed in flames, consuming Prometheus. A scream tore from Circe's throat before she could stop it.

Zeus whipped back, saw the flames and growled. "Fucking Argonauts." His gaze shot back to the battle where several Sirens were already on the ground, pinned by the Argonauts. "They're not going to win. Not this time."

He wrapped a hand around Circe's biceps and jerked her into him. "I still have you, witch."

* * * *

"Natasa..." Prometheus's eyes grew wide as the wall of flames surrounded him and his daughter drew close. "What are you doing here? How did you—"

She knelt at his feet and laid her hand over the chain at his ankles. "Titus figured out you were going to Olympus. We followed and found Circe's cave thanks to Cerek."

The chain grew red beneath her hand, and he hissed in a breath as the heat of the fire element inside her melted the adamant chain as if it were nothing. It broke open and dropped to the ground, freeing his legs. "But how—"

"I fanned the flames in her cauldron." Pushing to her feet, she grasped a piece of the rock wall sticking out and climbed two feet off the ground so she could place her hand over the chain above his right arm. "Her spell was still active. It showed me where to find you."

The chain above his head broke free. He dropped his arm, rolled his shoulder to stretch his sore muscles as she moved around him and did the same to the last chain pinning him to the rocks.

"Zeus set this all up," he said as the final chain melted, freeing him. He rubbed at his sore wrist, a growing panic rising in his chest. "He tricked her. He wants me to suffer, and he's using her to make that happen."

"I know." Natasa moved to stand in front of him, the wall of flames crackling around them a barrier even Zeus couldn't penetrate. "Which is why this just got a whole lot trickier. We'll only have one shot to get her away from Zeus."

His gaze narrowed. "What are you thinking?"

"Something that's only going to happen with Circe's help. How sure are you that she's on our side?"

* * * *

Circe fell against the hard wall of Zeus's chest with a grunt. Zeus's black eyes reflected the flames as he squeezed her upper arm, sending pain all through her biceps.

"You'll pay for this, witch," he growled. "You'll pay for all of this."

Her gaze shot to the flames as she felt Zeus's energy build around them. Zeus was going to flash them back to Olympus. Before she would ever know if Prometheus was alive or dead.

Panic clawed at her chest. "Titos," she whispered.

The wall of flames parted. Prometheus's large body launched through the opening and smacked into Zeus. The king of the gods jerked her forward, but the force of Prometheus's blow broke his hold on Circe, and she stumbled before finding her footing.

The two gods rolled across the ground, a tangle of arms and legs, swinging fists and bunching muscles. Zeus gathered electrical energy in his hand and zapped Prometheus's shoulder, causing the Titan to lurch back. Before he could zap Prometheus a second time, a fireball that seemed to come out of nowhere struck Zeus's hand, tearing a screech from Zeus's throat.

Circe's eyes grew wide, and she staggered back from the fight, from the flames. Her back hit something hard.

"Hold still," a female said behind her.

Warmth gathered around Circe's wrists, followed by a burn that cut across her skin. She cried out, but before the sound fully escaped her lips, the chains at her wrist fell to the ground, freeing her hands.

She whipped around and looked into Prometheus's daughter's eyes. "How did you—"

"We don't have time for that. These chains were forged by Hephaestus, correct?"

"Yes. They're made of adamant."

"So if we get them on Zeus, he won't be able to break free, will he?"

Circe saw where this was going. Grunts, the sounds of fists hitting bone, and blade clashing with blade, echoed around them. "Yes. Yes, that's right."

"Then do your thing and get them on Zeus's wrists." Natasa rushed past her, held out her hand. A fireball formed in her palm. She watched Zeus and Prometheus, rolling over the ground. When Zeus shifted on top, pinning Prometheus beneath him, Natasa launched the ball, hitting Zeus in the back. The god's shirt erupted in flames.

Zeus shrieked, released Prometheus, and lurched to his feet. Knowing this was her only shot, Circe held her hands over the chains that had just fallen from her wrists, closed her eyes, blocking out all that was happening around her, and summoned forth an attraction spell.

The chains rattled. Zeus growled somewhere close and said, "She'll die for this, Titan. She and your precious offspring will both die for what you've done here."

Circe's focus honed in on the chain, on the spell, and with the last uttered word, she felt the chain rise from the ground and shoot to her left.

"*Noooo!*" Zeus's shocked voice echoed in the air, followed by a *thwack* and a grunt.

Opening her eyes, Circe turned to look. The king of the gods lay on his back on the ground, his bound wrists shackled at his front.

"You can't do this. You can't!" Zeus screamed as Prometheus pushed to his feet, sweaty and dusty as he crossed to stand over the king of the gods. Zeus's dark eyes shimmered with retribution. "Sirens!"

"Oh, you mean those Sirens?" Prometheus angled his head to his left. Circe's gaze drifted to the battle—or what was left of it. Bows and daggers littered the ground out of reach of the six Sirens standing in a circle, surrounded by the Argonauts with weapons drawn, just in case. "They're out of commission."

Fury twisted Zeus's face. "You'll pay for this. Do you hear me? You and all the fucking Argoleans will pay."

"Not today we won't." Prometheus grasped Zeus by the arm and hefted the king of the gods to his feet. "Natasa?"

Prometheus's daughter rushed over and helped him maneuver Zeus to the rock wall where Prometheus had been chained.

"What are you doing?" Zeus's eyes grew so wide, the whites glowed all around his coal black irises as they jerked his arms over his head and chained him to the rocks. "What do you think you're doing? You can't leave me here."

"Can and will." Prometheus stepped back as Natasa latched the last chain to Zeus's feet. "You like torture so much, I think it's about time you got a taste of it yourself."

A screech echoed from the cave to their left. Zeus's eyes grew even wider as he looked in that direction, panic and true fear rushing over his features. "Release me. Release me right now!"

Natasa rose and stepped back. Looking toward her father, she said,

"We're good here. Go to her."

He squeezed his daughter's hand. Then turned to face Circe.

Circe's breath caught as Prometheus headed toward her. Dust covered his hair, his ripped shirt, and torn pants. A track of blood from a gash in his forehead stained his cheek but the wound was already sealing from his Titan genes. He stopped a foot away from her, and as he looked at her—really looked at her as he'd done in their gazebo—her heart sped up, tripping over itself until pain ricocheted all through her chest.

There were so many things she wanted to say to him, so many things she needed to make him understand. So many things she needed to make up for. "Titos, I—"

"Can you cast a spell on those Sirens so they think Zeus is dead?"

Confusion drew her brow together. That wasn't what she'd expected him to say. "Yes."

"Do it before that eagle comes out and we run out of time."

Turning away from him, she looked toward the Sirens and held out her hands. The Argonauts kept their weapons drawn but stepped back. She tuned out the sound of Zeus's continued threats, ignored the pain still burning her wrists from that melted chain, and tried not to be so aware of Prometheus standing close, but not close enough.

But as the cloaking spell fell from her lips, she knew she'd never be unaware of him. She cared for him. Would always care for him because he made her a better person.

"There," she said when the spell was done. "It's cast."

Prometheus looked toward the Argonauts, blocking the Sirens' view of Zeus, and nodded. Blinking, Circe watched as the Argonauts opened a portal and took the Sirens and Natasa through.

When the portal closed, she gathered her courage and turned to Prometheus. "I'm so sorry. I didn't mean for any of this to happen. I didn't mean for—"

He moved before she saw him. And when his mouth closed over hers and his hands encircled her wrists, lifting them to rest against his chest, she gasped.

The gasp turned to a sigh as he drew her into a kiss that finally felt...free.

"I'll kill you for this," Zeus screamed in a crazed voice. "I'll kill you all, do you hear me?" The ground shook, followed by another shriek, this one not from a god but from a beast. A giant, winged, sharp-beaked beast.

"Oh, fuuuuuck," Zeus hollered just before the sound of flesh tearing echoed in the air.

Circe never had time to look because she felt herself flying, and when Prometheus finally drew back from her lips and she looked up into his mesmerizing eyes, she realized she wasn't in a barren desert anymore. She was in her gazebo—*their* gazebo—surrounded by the lush green forests of Argolea.

She glanced around the familiar surrounding and listened to the soft trickle of water rolling over the rocks in the river below. "You brought us back here."

He let go of her wrists—wrists, she realized, that were no longer burned but healed from his magical hands—and slid his arms around her waist. "Seemed like the perfect place for both of us to start over. Together, if that's what you want."

Her gaze shifted back to his. Warmth gathered in her chest, pushing aside all the fear and doubt and longing she'd lived with for far too long. "I do want. Oh, do I want, Titos. But...the spell I cast on those Sirens won't last. Athena will be able to tell they're charmed. Zeus will be free before long."

"I don't care."

"You have to. He'll come after you. What will you do?"

"What I should have done a long time ago. Help the Argonauts find the water element so Zeus can't use the Orb."

Her heart swelled. He might be a Titan but he was every bit a hero as the Argonauts.

"We're safe here," he said, gazing down at her with soft eyes. Eyes she could see a future in. A real future. "Zeus can't cross into this realm, and his Sirens are no match for me...or us."

Her heart skipped a beat. "Are you sure you want me? Knowing everything you now know about me?"

A sexy half-smile curled his lips, and he tightened his arms around her waist, pulling her against the heat and life of his body. "Yes, I want you, Keia. In case you haven't noticed, we're the same, you and I. And the intensity with which I want you has not changed in the last day. If anything, it's only amplified."

She smiled because she definitely felt that intensity amplifying against her belly. "You won't grow tired of me? Witches aren't the easiest of beings to get along with."

"Neither are Titans." Flexing his hands against her lower spine, he pulled her in closer and leaned down toward her mouth. "But I have a feeling we have plenty of time to work all of that out."

They did. Sighing, she lifted to her toes and threaded her fingers through his silky dark hair as she opened to his kiss.

Thanks to him, nothing but eternity stretched before her, and she intended to spend every moment of it with him.

* * * *

Also from 1001 Dark Nights and Elisabeth Naughton, discover Ravaged.

Sign up for the 1001 Dark Nights Newsletter
and be entered to win a Tiffany Key necklace.

There's a contest every month!

Go to www.1001DarkNights.com to subscribe.

As a bonus, all subscribers will receive a free
1001 Dark Nights story
The First Night
by Lexi Blake & M.J. Rose

Turn the page for a full list of the
1001 Dark Nights fabulous novellas...

Discover 1001 Dark Nights Collection Three

HIDDEN INK by Carrie Ann Ryan
A Montgomery Ink Novella

BLOOD ON THE BAYOU by Heather Graham
A Cafferty & Quinn Novella

SEARCHING FOR MINE by Jennifer Probst
A Searching For Novella

DANCE OF DESIRE by Christopher Rice

ROUGH RHYTHM by Tessa Bailey
A Made In Jersey Novella

DEVOTED by Lexi Blake
A Masters and Mercenaries Novella

Z by Larissa Ione
A Demonica Underworld Novella

FALLING UNDER YOU by Laurelin Paige
A Fixed Trilogy Novella

EASY FOR KEEPS by Kristen Proby
A Boudreaux Novella

UNCHAINED by Elisabeth Naughton
An Eternal Guardians Novella

HARD TO SERVE by Laura Kaye
A Hard Ink Novella

DRAGON FEVER by Donna Grant
A Dark Kings Novella

KAYDEN/SIMON by Alexandra Ivy/Laura Wright
A Bayou Heat Novella

STRUNG UP by Lorelei James
A Blacktop Cowboys® Novella

MIDNIGHT UNTAMED by Lara Adrian
A Midnight Breed Novella

TRICKED by Rebecca Zanetti
A Dark Protectors Novella

DIRTY WICKED by Shayla Black
A Wicked Lovers Novella

A SEDUCTIVE INVITATION by Lauren Blakely
A Seductive Nights New York Novella

SWEET SURRENDER by Liliana Hart
A MacKenzie Family Novella

For more information, visit www.1001DarkNights.com.

Discover 1001 Dark Nights Collection One

FOREVER WICKED by Shayla Black
CRIMSON TWILIGHT by Heather Graham
CAPTURED IN SURRENDER by Liliana Hart
SILENT BITE: A SCANGUARDS WEDDING by Tina Folsom
DUNGEON GAMES by Lexi Blake
AZAGOTH by Larissa Ione
NEED YOU NOW by Lisa Renee Jones
SHOW ME, BABY by Cherise Sinclair
ROPED IN by Lorelei James
TEMPTED BY MIDNIGHT by Lara Adrian
THE FLAME by Christopher Rice
CARESS OF DARKNESS by Julie Kenner

Also from 1001 Dark Nights

TAME ME by J. Kenner

For more information, visit www.1001DarkNights.com.

Discover 1001 Dark Nights Collection Two

WICKED WOLF by Carrie Ann Ryan
WHEN IRISH EYES ARE HAUNTING by Heather Graham
EASY WITH YOU by Kristen Proby
MASTER OF FREEDOM by Cherise Sinclair
CARESS OF PLEASURE by Julie Kenner
ADORED by Lexi Blake
HADES by Larissa Ione
RAVAGED by Elisabeth Naughton
DREAM OF YOU by Jennifer L. Armentrout
STRIPPED DOWN by Lorelei James
RAGE/KILLIAN by Alexandra Ivy/Laura Wright
DRAGON KING by Donna Grant
PURE WICKED by Shayla Black
HARD AS STEEL by Laura Kaye
STROKE OF MIDNIGHT by Lara Adrian
ALL HALLOWS EVE by Heather Graham
KISS THE FLAME by Christopher Rice
DARING HER LOVE by Melissa Foster
TEASED by Rebecca Zanetti
THE PROMISE OF SURRENDER by Liliana Hart

Also from 1001 Dark Nights

THE SURRENDER GATE By Christopher Rice
SERVICING THE TARGET By Cherise Sinclair

For more information, visit www.1001DarkNights.com.

About Elisabeth Naughton

Before topping multiple bestseller lists--including those of the New York Times, USA Today, and the Wall Street Journal--Elisabeth Naughton taught middle school science. A voracious reader, she soon discovered she had a knack for creating stories with a chemistry of their own. The spark turned into a flame, and Naughton now writes full-time. Besides topping bestseller lists, her books have been nominated for some of the industry's most prestigious awards, such as the RITA® and Golden Heart Awards from Romance Writers of America, the Australian Romance Reader Awards, and the Golden Leaf Award. When not dreaming up new stories, Naughton can be found spending time with her husband and three children in their western Oregon home. Learn more at www.ElisabethNaughton.com.

Discover Elisabeth Naughton

Ravaged
An Eternal Guardians Novella
By Elisabeth Naughton

Ari — *Once an Eternal Guardian, now he's nothing but a rogue mercenary with one singular focus: revenge.*

His guardian brothers all think he's dead, but Ari is very much alive in the human realm, chipping away at Zeus's Sirens every chance he can, reveling in his brutality and anonymity. Until, that is, he abducts the wrong female and his identity is finally exposed. It will take more than the Eternal Guardians, more even than the gods to rein Ari in after everything he's done. It may just take the courage of one woman willing to stand up to a warrior who's become a savage.

* * * *

Daphne darted a look between Zeus and Athena, sure she had to have heard them wrong. "What you need from me?"

Athena shot a frustrated look at Zeus, but the king of the gods didn't bother to glance the goddess's way. "We're in need of a Siren with your talents to complete a mission for us. Are you interested?"

Daphne had no idea what kind of mission they were talking about, but something in her gut said never to say no to the king of the gods. "Yes, of course."

"She's too naïve," Athena mumbled.

"That's exactly why we're going to use her." Zeus's eyes flashed.

"You've heard of the rogue Argonaut loose in the human realm? The one they call Ari?"

Daphne's mind skipped over snippets of gossip she'd heard from her Siren sisters. "We all have. He's a monster."

"Yes, he is." Zeus's jaw clenched. "A very dangerous monster that needs to be stopped. Unfortunately, our conventional attempts at dealing with him have not worked. Which is where you come in. We want to send you in undercover to terminate him for the Order."

Daphne stared at the god for several seconds, sure she had to have heard him wrong. "Me? But I-I'm not even a Siren yet. I haven't taken my final vows. I'm—"

"You are a nymph. A voluptuous, alluring nymph, like your mother. Aristokles has but one weakness: sexy, vulnerable nymphs. You will pretend to be in jeopardy, let him take you back to his lair, and when he least expects it, kill him."

Daphne's heart beat hard, and her hands grew sweaty. This was a suicide mission. She'd heard horror stories about the crazed Argonaut and what he liked to do to Sirens. "But...my king...he tortures and kills Sirens. I'll not make it past—"

"You are not a full Siren yet," Athena cut in. "You have not been inducted, you do not bear the marking, and because of your nymph heritage, your body was never altered. He will not sense that you are a Siren, because you are not one...yet."

"If you succeed in this mission, however," Zeus added, "you will be inducted immediately upon your return. Regardless of your marksmanship scores."

Daphne's pulse roared in her head. This was her chance to belong. To finally be one of them. Her stomach swirled with excitement and apprehension. "Wh-what would I need to do?"

"Kill him, of course," Zeus answered. "But before you do that, I need confirmation of something. I suspect the Argonaut has a very special marking on his body. Not the Argonaut markings on his forearms. This is something else. Before he's terminated, I need you to search his entire body and either prove or disprove the appearance of the marking."

"What kind of marking?" Daphne asked.

Zeus glanced toward Athena. A silent look passed between the two gods before Zeus refocused on Daphne. "We're not sure. But the marking disappears at the time of death, so you cannot kill him and then look for it. You must find it while he is alive."

So all she had to do was get close enough to the mass-murdering psycho to check every inch of his skin for some unknown marking. Yeah. That sounded easy.

Not.

"I-I'm not sure how I would do that," Daphne said hesitantly.

"This is where your nymph background comes in handy." Zeus lifted his brows in a "duh, it's easy" move. "Use your seduction skills. Charm him. Get him to drop his guard. Earn his trust so he least suspects your mission."

A whir echoed in Daphne's ears. "You don't mean—"

"Yes, you'll have to screw him," Athena said. "Probably several times." An irritated expression crossed the goddess's face. "You sailed through seduction training, Daphne. This shouldn't be that difficult for you."

Unease rippled through Daphne. She'd only been twenty when she'd been plucked from her foster home and brought to Olympus to train with the Sirens. Barely old enough to come into her sexuality, and the males she'd fooled around with as a teenager didn't count. Yes, she'd made it through seduction training easily, but only because she'd had an amazing instructor, a minor god who hadn't forced her. One who'd taken plenty of time to teach her about her own body and the powers of sex. That didn't mean she had any real experience seducing males—

she'd been here for seven years, for crying out loud. And she had zero experience with savages like the psycho Argonaut Aristokles.

"We need an answer," Zeus said. "Either you are with us—"

"Or you are without us," Athena finished.

Daphne's gaze slid from one god to the other. She knew what they were saying. Either she did this and became a full-fledged Siren, or she didn't and was banished from the Order forever.

"Well?" Zeus asked.

Sickness rolled through her stomach. Her small village in Thrace was gone. Her parents long dead. She had no family left, no home, nothing to turn to if she lost the Sirens. Which meant she had to make this work.

Swallowing back the fear, Daphne nodded and prayed she made it through this alive. "I'll do it."

On behalf of 1001 Dark Nights,
Liz Berry and M.J. Rose would like to thank ~

Steve Berry
Doug Scofield
Kim Guidroz
Jillian Stein
InkSlinger PR
Dan Slater
Asha Hossain
Chris Graham
Pamela Jamison
Jessica Johns
Dylan Stockton
Richard Blake
BookTrib After Dark
The Dinner Party Show
and Simon Lipskar

9514

Made in the USA
Lexington, KY
13 June 2016